THE NAVY OF MANKIND: WASP SQUADRON

BOOK 2

CRYSTALS

Colonel Jonathan P. Brazee
USMC (Ret)

A Semper Fi Press Book

Copyright © 2018 Jonathan Brazee

ISBN-13: 978-1-945743-24-5
ISBN-10: 1-945743-24-7 (Semper Fi Press)

Printed in the United States of America

Acknowledgements:
I want to thank all those who took the time to offer advice as I wrote this book. A special shout-out goes to real Navy air warriors, CAPT Andrés "Drew" Brugal, USN, (Ret) and CAPT Timothy "Spike" Prendergast, USN (Ret.) for keeping helping me with "air-speak" and culture, and to my beta readers James Caplan, Kelly O'Donnell, and Micky Cocker for their valuable input.

Cover by Jude Beers

DEDICATION

Airman Joel C. Loftus, USAF
KIA 7 June 1969
Phan Rang Air Base, Republic of Vietnam

SG-88218

Chapter 1

"Keep it together, *Tala* girl," Beth said as her fighter took another hit.

She reached up to adjust her head's-up, banging her elbow, on the . . . heck, she didn't know what it was. She had thought things were tight when she and Bull had shared a cockpit after the fight in the SG-9222 system, but this was ridiculous. Every cubic centimeter inside her cockpit was crammed with instruments.

Three alien fighters were on the *Tala*, closing the range as they tried to destroy her. The lead fighter was 28 kiloklicks away, which was too close for comfort. She was extremely aware of the G-shot trigger, and she ached to fire it and get the hell out of Dodge, but her mission was vital.

She took another pulse of an alien beam weapon—at least the eggheads had figured out that much. During her second encounter with the aliens—her first as a Wasp pilot— her instruments could detect that something had fired at them, but they lacked the sophistication to identify just what it was. It wasn't until they'd returned and the scientists got their hands on the data that they began to make much sense of things.

Not enough sense, however, which was why Petty Officer Third Class Floribeth Salinas O'Shea Dalisay, Navy of Humankind, was in this remote, unexplored system, playing target for the three alien craft. They didn't even know enough to have a name for them. Officially, they were designated NSB-1's, for Nonhuman Sentient Being-Ones, but despite a flurry of military nicknames being offered, none had stuck so far. It was hard to name an alien race if no one even knew what they looked like yet.

The aliens seemed to have three weapons. Their torpedo was pretty easy to understand. Round where the Navy torpedoes were cylindrical, they acted in much the same manner. They had two energy beam weapons. One seemed to be in line with the Navy's meson beam cannons—at least as exhibited by the Bremsstrahlung radiation. The other was different, possibly a microwave-type weapon.

Before the Navy risked any of its capital ships, they had to know just what they faced. And that was why Beth was letting the alien fighters engage her. She had to let the instruments crammed inside her Wasp analyze what was being fired at her, hopefully before they could register a kill—her.

If she were killed, the Navy would still get their data— they had made sure all of the instrumentation was broadcasting out through the gate she'd used to enter the system. Great for them, not so much for her. Mercy said it would probably be better if the *Tala* were destroyed—then the Navy would know just what it took to collapse her shields.

Beth had elbowed her friend in the side at that, leaving her gasping between laughs.

She took another hit as she juked. At this close distance, she couldn't dodge one of the alien beam weapons, but by constantly maneuvering, she hoped she was throwing off their targeting systems. Fire enough times, however, and they were going to connect, and each hit degraded her shielding further.

"OK, time to dish something back," she said, hitting her port thrusters.

She was already at .72C and not accelerating, so it didn't matter what her aspect was to the pursuing fighters. The *Tala* rotated around and faced the enemy so she could fire her torpedoes. The torps could be fired in any direction—they'd lock in on their target and then maneuver as necessary, but a head-on shot gave the most direct route.

She acquired the target and fired. Over that short of a distance, a torpedo would normally reach the target within seconds, but both *Tala* and the torp were still heading away at .72 C, so even with the pursuing aliens approaching, it took longer. Beth watched her displays, hoping she could at least rack up one kill, but the torp was destroyed before it hit.

"I hope you got all of that," she said to the unseen scientists back in human space.

A Wasp normally carried three torpedoes, but for this mission, Beth only had one—the rest of the magazine carried yet more instruments.

She'd spun back around, facing front, and a flurry of nano-pulses hit her. Her rear-facing shields dropped from 54% to 22%. It was getting to be crunch time, and she was still out of position.

"Why did you volunteer for this, Floribeth Salinas?" she muttered as she studied her array.

There hadn't been any question as to that, however. The commander had insisted that he was going to take the mission, but he barely fit in the cockpit as it was. With all the instruments the R&D science-types wanted to fit into a Wasp, there wasn't much room for a norm, much less a GT. And as the smallest pilot in the squadron, it was a no-brainer that she take the mission.

"Fox-four, you're down to 22%. Initiate retrograde," a steady voice came over the comms.

No shit.

"Roger that," she said instead. "I'm still two minutes out."

Two minutes in a dog fight might as well be forever. Even it they didn't continue to degrade her shields with energy weapons, she could be taken out by one of the aliens' torpedoes long before that. She wondered why they hadn't fired one yet, and for a moment, she wondered if they were testing her just as she was testing them.

No, no way. How could they know I'd show up here?

With billions of stars in the galaxy, most of it was still a vast unknown. Humans had seen signs of the NSB-1's before— they just hadn't known what those signs meant. Now that the aliens were a known entity, it hadn't been too difficult to locate the three fighters and put up a gate for her to pass through.

The three enemy fighters had to have spotted her as she burst into the system, and they had herded her like Australian shepherds to keep her away from that gate and her way back home. That had been expected, however. What hadn't been expected was how quickly they'd closed the range with her. If she wanted to get back to human space, she had to figure out a way to keep in one piece for a while longer.

She'd already absorbed a lot of damage. If this had been the first mission on SG-9222, she'd be dead now. Luckily, the *Tala* had been given upgraded shielding, which had kept the ship intact so far, but that also created its own problem. Designed for much larger ships, the heat buildup was having an effect on the *Tala's* efficiency.

Space might be bitterly cold, but without air, convection was almost non-existent. The heat could not escape and kept building up. Still, the science-types had assured her she could handle the heat build-up far better than what was turning out to be the reality. The shields were protecting her, but they might also end up cooking her.

Behind her, the three ships splayed out in a triangle. Something hit her hard, with much more power than anything before.

"The suckers are merging their fire," she shouted as she broke hard right.

Her shield was down to 8%. Another hit would be her last. Her finger poised over the G-shot trigger, but she'd just gotten out of her recuperation from the last time, and she didn't want to go through that again.

She checked a coordinate in space just ahead of her. If she could hold on 45 more seconds . . .

She wasn't going to hold on ten seconds like she was now. She adjusted her track and hit a final boost, then spun back around to face the three enemy fighters. Hopefully, that would give them pause for a moment, thinking that she had another torpedo. More importantly, it presented her fore shields. They weren't the souped-up shields she just had installed, but they were better than those now drawn down to 8%.

The aliens' formation adjusted, each point moving outwards from the others, and that gave Beth a few seconds of blessed relief. She watched her timer click down, trying to will it to move faster. At 22 seconds, the aliens fired, again, and the shield flared in a blue-white corona, illuminating her cockpit. Her eyes went to her readout—the front shields had dropped to 72% with one hit.

She'd made her move, and now, she couldn't maneuver. She simply had to bear up to whatever they could throw at her. Another shot played across her shielding and just like that, she was at 54%. She felt vulnerable as she sat facing the the enemy, out there somewhere in the black. She couldn't see them with her naked eyes, and on her display, they were mere blips. She certainly couldn't see the weapon fire until they splashed across her shield with a flash of light.

Beth jumped as the next round hit her, but the *Tala* kept going. She refused to check her display, afraid of what she'd see.

"This had better be worth it," she said aloud as she waited for the next shot, the one that might break her Wasp apart.

She'd already recorded a message to her ina and the rest of the family back on New Cebu, but in her heart, she hadn't thought that Mercy would have to send it. Now, it looked like her family was going to have to go it alone without her. At least the Navy would give them a hefty payment, far more than Hamdani Brothers would have paid had she bought it on one of their exploration missions.

Two flares, one after the other, hit her front, and she thought she could smell something burning—which was impossible with her helmet on and sealed. She told herself not to look, but like a magnet, the display dragged her eyes over: 7%.

Her silver cross was inside her flight suit and inaccessible. She reached up to where it lay against her chest and touched the spot, then lifted her fingers to her faceshield and kissed air. It didn't give her the same comfort as if she'd really kissed her cross, but it was better than nothing.

"Gate ahead," Rose said in the cool and steady voice Beth programmed into it.

"How long?" she yelled.

"Nine seconds . . . eight . . ."

Not enough time! One more shot and I'm dead!

As soon as Beth entered the system, a second gate had been opened, and a tiny gate drone sent through. It had waited, heavily shielded, ready to deploy a mini-gate once Beth got close enough. The hope was that the aliens would focus on the gate through which she'd entered the system and not on a yet-to-be-deployed gate, one just big enough for a Wasp.

"Take us through, Rose," she said, trusting her AI to match up the trajectory.

Bull had managed to survive a dead Wasp, so maybe she could, too. She waited for the flash, but her alarms went off instead.

They'd fired a torpedo!

One more beam, and she'd have been dead, but the aliens had seen the gate appear, and they must not have known what dire straits she'd been in, so they'd gone for a torpedo to ensure the kill.

". . . four . . . three . . ."

The torp was screaming, closing the gap as if she were standing still.

". . . two . . . one . . . gate."

"TORPEDO!" Beth shouted over the net as she shot into the midst of 16 Wasps and a monitor. "Break, break, break!"

The gate was to be destroyed the instant she passed through, but fire converged on her, the *Tala's* display lighting up like a Christmas tree. The torpedo must have made it through, too. Still flying backward, she saw the brief flash of light as it exploded, taken out by the combined fire of the fighters and the heavy monitor. If she could see the light like that, it had to have been very, very close. She didn't even check, afraid to see just how close.

She swiveled back around and started slowing down as she passed her squadron mates.

"Did you have to bring back one of the bad guys with you?" Mercy asked over the 1P.

"Yeah, I'm happy to see you, too."

SIERRA STATION

Chapter 2

Beth sat in the *Tala* as the tractor brought her into the hangar. She just wanted to get out of her Wasp as soon as possible. Her little Hummingbird had been cramped, and she'd spent upwards of 60 days on exploration missions in it, but she'd gotten used to what might be a tight squeeze for the other pilots but was positively spacious for her. With all the instrumentation crammed into the *Tala* now, however, it was much worse, and she couldn't even stretch her short legs out to their fullest.

The second she touched the deck, Beth retracted her canopy and started wiggling out.

"Careful!" someone shouted. "Freeze."

Beth wasn't sure who was shouting, so she kept extracting herself.

"I said stop, pilot! Don't move," a woman in civilian silver overalls said, coming alongside the *Tala*, followed by a small gaggle of more civilians.

"What?" Beth asked stupidly.

"Freeze. Do not move. We'll get you out."

Beth had already wiggled partially out, and now she had to stop, hands on the edge of the cockpit, supporting her weight. A Wasp was normally low-slung to the ground, but at 137 centimeters, Beth had to use the depressions that appeared in the *Tala's* fuselage whenever the canopy was retracted. Now, to her embarrassment, the civilian crew was wheeling up a platform and hoist, the type used when equipment modules were loaded into the cockpit.

As soon as the hoist reached her, she reached up for it, only to be chastised by a young man who said he'd get her out. She waited, already half-out, and her face reddened as he carefully reached around her with straps, then connected them.

"OK, I'm going to slowly raise you clear. Mind your feet, and don't kick anything."

What the . . . she wondered. *They're worried that I'm going to hurt one of their precious pieces of equipment? I just took them through combat, for Pete's sake!*

She shut up as the hoist pulled her free—and she immediately spun around, feet up in the air and head pointed at the deck. She caught a glimpse of Mercy climbing out of her Wasp, pointing at her and laughing.

The hoist swung about and lowered her as hands reached up to right her and land her on her feet, which did nothing for her ego. She could take the *Tala* into enemy-held space, let them fire at her willy-nilly, but evidently, she was not capable enough to make it from the cockpit to the hangar deck on her own.

One of the sets of hands helping her was Seaman Josh Fry, her plane captain. As soon as the straps holding her were released and the civilians turned their attention back to her Wasp, she reached up and pulled the taller sailor down to her level.

"Keep an eagle-eye on them. I don't want the *Tala* destroyed while they recover their equipment."

"And I don't want to spend a month repairing anything they do. Don't worry. I'm on it," he said, casting a worried look at the people swarming the *Tala*.

She knew he would. He'd been made her plane captain so she'd be senior to him, but she'd rather have him over any of the others. The *Tala* was probably more his baby than she was hers.

"That was pretty graceful," Mercy said, walking up to her.

"Eat me."

"Good job, though," her friend said, suddenly serious. "I was . . . I was . . ."

"Yeah, me, too," Beth said, accepting Mercy's hug. "It was close."

And then the rest of the pilots were there, congratulating her and slapping her back. She was bombarded with questions until the commander came to the rescue.

"Let her be for now. She's got a debrief in ten, so at least let her get a Coke first," he said.

There was a rumble of laughter. Beth's penchant for Coke was something of a running joke. As if on cue, Seaman Apprentice Glorya Leung, with whom Beth had spent more than a few working parties, came running up with a cold pressure-pouch of Coke.

"Thanks, Glorya," she said, taking it with gratitude.

As the junior-most pilot in the squadron, and the only pilot with two kills, she'd become somewhat of a favorite among the other junior enlisted sailors.

She squeezed the top open and took a long draught.

Oh, man, that's good, she thought, suddenly relieved that she'd made it back in one piece.

A shudder ran through her as it hit her that she'd come close to never tasting another Coke, never having another burger or stargrinder again. She was lucky—for the second time. She couldn't count on luck to get her out of jams—at some point, her luck was going to run out.

"You ready?" Commander Tuominen asked.

"Yes, sir."

"Well, they're waiting, so, let's get this over."

"I'll catch you later," Beth mouthed at Mercy as she followed the squadron commander out of the hangar bay.

Her bunkmate nodded, then blew her a kiss.

She wasn't looking forward to the next however-many-hours. The key to the mission was what had already been transmitted back and what could be gleaned from the instruments themselves. Still, the command couldn't stand by and let civilians, even Navy employees, run the show, and they controlled Beth. There wasn't much she could tell them that they couldn't see from her black box, but she was beginning to understand the Navy system by now. By taking her debrief, even if it wouldn't reveal anything useful or new, they were asserting their command and control. It was just one of those things that simply had to be endured.

It would have been nice if I could have taken a shower first and gotten a bite to eat.

She had a feeling that it was going to be a long time before she had a free moment again.

****

At five hours, the debrief after returning from the mission had been shorter than she'd expected. There had even been food: sandwiches and fruit sticks. She'd almost laughed to see stargrinders on the sandwich platter, as if the mess chief had read her mind.

Still, it had been a pain in the butt, even with the commander there to carry part of the load. The problem was that the commander hadn't been in the system with her, so most of what was asked was up to her to answer, and every captain and the two admirals seemed bound and determined to make sure they were listed in the debrief records, even if they asked the same question someone else asked not five minutes before.

There was one highlight. At the conclusion, Rear Admiral Waverly had casually reminded his aide to makes sure the "award recommendation" had been submitted.

Military people were not supposed to strive for awards, but as Napoleon said, "A soldier will fight long and hard for a bit of colored ribbon." As an exploration scout with Hamdani Brothers, her reward was her salary, nothing more. Since joining the Navy, however, the ribbons worn by the others had taken on a degree of importance—and if she could admit it to herself, she coveted them, being painfully aware of her bare chest. Very secure with herself in most ways, she still went through life with a bit of a chip on her shoulder, always having to prove herself. A ribbon, as trivial as that might seem to a civilian, was also a mark of credibility.

She knew she'd been recommended for an award for her first action against the aliens, but if she were going to get something for this mission, that would be two ribbons. That wouldn't be close to CWO5 Mbatu's eight, but it was a start.

That first debrief had been something to endure, but today's, five days later, was going to be different. If this debrief went for five hours, she didn't care. One, she wasn't speaking. Two, she was damned curious as to what the science-types had discovered. She knew that this would only be some preliminary findings, but that was better than nothing. She'd faced the enemy three times now, and she didn't have a clue as to who . . . or what . . . they were.

"I'm still betting they're gaseous—" Mercy said before being cut off by Jim Caplan, a First Class petty officer just six months from qualifying to make the jump to warrant officer.

"Yeah, so you can call them farts," he said.

Mercy started to protest, but Beth said, "That wasn't funny the first 99 times you told us that."

"Yes, it is! You guys just can't appreciate good humor."

Mercy had a, well, *weird*, sense of humor, was the best way Beth could describe it. Beth loved her to death, but her jokes sucked, and she would usually be the only one to laugh when she told them.

She was also a fearless pilot, as she'd proven before. In pilot-speak, Beth knew that Mercy "had her six."

After Swordfish—Lieutenant Hadley—had been killed, and with Beth going through rehab, the future of Fox Flight had been somewhat up in the air, and Beth didn't even know if she'd be returned to the flight. The commander ended up sending Warthog to be the flight leader of Hotel while waiting for Bull, Uncle, and Ranger to get through rehab. He left Mercy in Fox and sent over Capgun (Jim Caplan) as they awaited a new Lieutenant Commander, Seth "Gollum" Vestergaard, to arrive and become flight leader.

She was pretty happy with the new Fox Flight. Capgun was an outstanding pilot, and he had one kill, tallied during the Syngenta Enclave. Along with Beth's two kills, that matched the tally of the rest of the squadron combined.

The commander had only been with the squadron for a week—he hadn't taken part in the mission, but he had been a flight instructor, so his skills were unquestioned. The other three were still trying to feel him out as a leader, but so far, he seemed OK.

"Here they come," Beth said as a mixed group of half-a-dozen civilians and sailors came into the classroom.

Immediately, what had been a low murmur of conversations died off. Everyone wanted to hear this.

The head scientist was a GT with a light rose skin coloration, a head taller than the commodore, who had stepped to the front and faced the room as if he was going to talk before she perfunctorily cut him off.

"I am Doctor Jessica One Off, and I've agreed to present you with an initial assessment of the NSB-1's. This is highly perfunctory at this stage, but I deem it appropriate as you gathered the data at no small risk to yourselves, and if necessary, you will face NSB-1's before a full assessment is completed, any knowledge, no matter how incomplete, may be beneficial."

Two things stood out by her statements. First, she was from the One Off clan, one of the more powerful GT families. Second, she used the "doctor" title, instead of the more commonly used "Mzee" for members of the Golden Tribe.

GT's came in two flavors: the grandees who lived their lives of luxury and pursuit of the latest trends, and those who believed in a productive life. As a child on New Cebu, Beth had assumed all GTs led the lives of ease as depicted in the holovids, but they would never have taken control of humanity unless some of them actually ran things. Doctor One Off was obviously one of those who felt the need to work.

Over the stage projector, a three-meter-long ship appeared to the oohs and ahs of the pilots and selected staff. It had the overall appearance of a crystal formation that one might find in a cave somewhere, all haphazard-looking angles and without the clean lines of most modern human ships.

The doctor looked up from her pad, obviously surprised at the outburst of sound. She scrunched her perfect lilac eyebrows in confusion.

"Yes, that is an NSB-1 ship," she said, then paused a moment as if realizing the impact the image was having on them.

Beth knew that she had intended to jump right into their findings, not understanding how the image would affect those in the room. That, right there, was the enemy. Not a blip on a screen. The real deal. All of the sailors in the room were either pilots or in the business of keeping fighters spaceworthy, and their minds were aligned with things that crossed the black. This was the first time they'd seen a ship that was not made by humans, and the sight had captured their attention like nothing else could.

"Now, I will continue," she said after a short ten seconds. "None of our instrumentation was able to pierce the physical structure of the three NSB-1 ships, so we still do not know the make-up, or even if, there are pilots or crew onboard."

"Farts," Mercy whispered to Beth, who elbowed her hard in the ribs.

"More on that to come, but for the present, you will notice that this arrangement of crystalline fractals significantly increases the surface area given a like volume. There can be many reasons for this configuration, and we have not definitively determined why the NSB-1's ships are in this form, but the reason with the most potential to reflect reality is that the fractals are heat dumps."

All ships that plied the black had heat sinks in some form or another. If heat could readily be dissipated through conduction and convection in space, then ships would be round as the most economical shape for a given payload. However, heat has to be bled off, so other shapes with more surface area were used. Some stations, particularly manufacturers where large amounts of heat were generated, had radiators as large as their solar panels, with kilometers of tubing filled with ammonia used to transport huge amounts of heat from the station to the radiators. The Navy Wasp was a dual space/atmosphere ship, so its shape had to take into account aerodynamics, but the designers still had to design an ATCS, or an Active Thermal Control System, to take into account heat buildup caused by everything from the powerful FC engine to the pilot's own body heat.

"The reason behind our preliminary conclusions goes beyond mere conjecture. One of the three weapons systems, which we have designated AWS-2, makes use of heat. But let me digress for a moment first. AWS-1 is a hadron beam energy weapon, one almost indistinguishable from human systems."

A mass of numbers and calculations appeared over the holo of the enemy ship.

"Commodore Charpentier has assured me that those of you gathered here are not interested in the specific calculations, but I believe him to be mistaken."

"Satan's balls! She just shaded the commodore," Mercy whispered as the commodore couldn't keep the corners of his mouth from turning down.

"If you look at the zeta . . ."

The doctor went on for at least five minutes, four-minutes-and-fifty-five seconds of which Beth was lost. She just stared at the holo of the alien ship, imagining getting weapons lock on it. All she took from the doctor's lecture was that the alien's beamer was essentially the same as a human beam weapon, and that was good enough for her. She didn't have to know how to make a Wasp, after all—she just had to know how to fly it.

"So, that brings us to AWS-2. This would fall under the category of a yet undetermined type of micro-wave, but with some significant differences. We are not sure how it actually works, but by examining the hull of FT6X-079 . . ."

Beth sat up straighter. FT6X-079 was the hull designation of the *Tala*.

" . . . we can see significant damage on a molecular level due to heat."

Damage? Does Josh know? Can he fix it?

"With some slight adjustments by the NSB-1 weapons system, zeroing in to an optimum frequency, we believe that

FT6X-079 would have been destroyed early on in the engagement . . ."

Not just the ship, lady. I was in the Tala at the time, in case you forgot.

Mercy squeezed her hand. She hadn't missed that small little point, either.

". . . and we believe that the NSB-1 pilot, if they have pilots, was attempting to do just that. The incremental damage was spread over what we deduce would have been different and ranging bandwidths."

They were testing us, just like we were testing them.

"If we accept the possibility that ASW-2 is in fact a heat-based weapons system of a type humanity has not developed, then it becomes intuitively obvious to the casual observer that the fractals in the NSB-1 vessels are potentially heat exchangers. Once again, the caveat is that this theory is just that, a theory, one that must be rigorously tested before we can claim accuracy."

"Does that mean more missions where we're target practice?" Mercy asked. "That's easy for her to say."

"That leads us to ASW-3, the torpedo. Thanks to a fortuitous turn of events, we were able to recover a multitude of fragments of the one that passed through the gate. And here, despite the fact that it is very similar to human-made weapons, secondary evidence has proven to be quite interesting and, dare I say, valuable?"

More figures appeared over the holo of the ship, and the doctor went deep into science-speak, almost all of it over Beth's head. She had no idea what "regressive etchings" or "stepped analytics" meant, and she surreptitiously looked around to see if she was the only one who was lost. As a child of the barangay whose highest pinnacle of success would have been becoming a domestic on another planet, education had been a luxury that her family couldn't afford. She was relieved to see that the university-educated pilots all had glazed eyes as well.

A collective gasp filled the room, however, pulling Beth back to the briefing, and it dawned on her what the doctor had just said. Somehow, all the regressive etchings and the rest had indicated something about the aliens, and it was a doozy.

The torpedo components had been exposed to chlorine for an extended period of time. The most logical explanation was that the aliens were chlorine-breathers.

Chapter 4

"Shh, here he comes," Mercy whispered before Beth dug her fingers into her friend's thigh under the table.

"Just act normal," Beth said out of the corner of her mouth before waving NSP3 Tantamount Lister over. "We saved you a spot," she told him as he looked around the galley, tray in hand.

"Hurl" nodded and approached, gratefully taking a seat. Beth loved Hurl—because of him, she was no longer the junior pilot in the squadron, and the command master chief had a new best friend. Hurl had already been put in charge of three head-cleaning details in the six days since he'd arrived.

With Hurl and NSP1 Diania Park, there were now 15 enlisted pilots in the squadron, still a minority, and still not totally accepted by the more senior officer pilots. Part of that was jealousy, Capgun thought. As an enlisted pilot, even if she made warrant officer, Beth would never do anything else. The commissioned officers had to alternate flying billets with shore billets, all the better to make "rounded" leaders if they got selected for command. This was only Commander Tuominen's second flight billet, although his position was unique, and not because he was a GT. As the head of the developmental squadron that came up with contingency plans should another space-going lifeform be found, he was the logical choice to head up VFX-99. The question was if they'd allow him to keep it if—no, *when*—things got hot.

Hurl might be a fellow swabbie, but that didn't mean he was going to get a free pass from the rest of them. Mercy gave out a half-snort, half-laugh as he sat down, earning her another thigh-squeeze. Hurl didn't seem to notice, instead poking at his plate for a moment.

"At least the chow here's pretty good," he said, taking a forkful of the yakisoba and studying it for a moment before popping it into his mouth. "Our food at Resolute sucked big time."

"You're not on Resolute anymore, Hurl," Mercy said with the disdain most pilots had for ground-based sailors. Heck, they were almost as bad as Marines. "And thank your lucky stars for that."

Hurl had become a pilot through a round-about path, being a heavy equipment operator in a naval engineering brigade, building the new base on Resolute. He'd been pulled after annual sim-tests and given the opportunity to go to flight school. Sim-tests can only indicate so much, however. His reflexes were off-the-charts—his stomach not so much. He'd almost been dropped after exhibiting a propensity for vomiting in zero-G, something that was finally conquered with a drug cocktail. Unfortunately for him, though, his "Hurl" callsign had been forwarded to the squadron by the flight school instructors, and it had been cemented in place even before he arrived—much to his chagrin.

Beth almost felt sorry for him—with heavy emphasis on the "almost." He was still the boot pilot, and forms had to be followed.

"You feeling comfortable? Stable?" Mercy asked after Hurl had taken a few bites.

"Yeah, why?" he asked, brows scrunched together in confusion.

"Oh, nothing," she said, trying to cut off a laugh.

Beth tried not to roll her eyes. As a partner in crime, Mercy was not good in the execution. She had the ideas, too many of them, but that was about it.

"So, when do you get your Wasp? Any word yet?"

"No," he said, frowning. "Still on hold."

The debrief by Doctor One Off had only been two weeks ago, and the squadron was on a semi-grounded status. Half of the Wasps were kept on an alert status while the engineers and scientists argued how to best retrofit the fighters in order to meet the threat. That meant the neither Hurl, Park, or Ensign Kigusiuq, the other new join, had been assigned a frame yet. It was probably driving them crazy.

"Don't worry. Soon, you'll get your Wasp and be out plying the black," she said.

"If he ever gets off his ass, that is," Mercy said

Beth jabbed her friend hard in the ribs, keeping an expressionless face toward Hurl, who looked confused by Mercy's statement.

"It's not my fault. I'm there every day to check status," he said, misunderstanding her meaning. He shifted uncomfortably in his seat, and his confusion turned into . . . more confusion as he looked down at his lap. "What the . . . ?"

Mercy lost it, her braying laugh filling the galley. Others turned to see what had set her off. Across the table, Hurl tried to get up, but he was stuck. Even using his arms to push up, he wasn't moving.

"I can't move," he said, stating the obvious.

"Ooh, I guess a little weldbond would do that," Beth said.

"What? You put . . . you put weldbond on my overalls?"

"On your seat. You put them on your overalls when you sat down."

"Mother fucking . . ." he went on with an impressive string of curses as he strained to break free.

"Satan's balls, Hurl, such language," Mercy said as the rest of the galley, realizing what was happening, joined in the laughter.

He struggled for a few more minutes, but Navy overalls were made to be impervious to wear and tear aboard a ship, and once weldbond set, it was virtually impossible to break the weld without the debonder (which Beth had but wasn't going to volunteer that fact).

"OK, OK, you got me. Ha, ha," he said sarcastically. "Good one. Now how the hell am I going to leave?"

Beth was about to take pity on him when Mercy said, "You can't like that. You've got to get out of your overalls."

"I can't," he said in a whisper, leaning across the table as far as he could go. "I'm going commando."

Commando? What does he mean? Beth wondered for a moment before she realized what he meant. *Oh, that does cause a problem.*

She reached for the debonder, but Mercy grabbed her forearm and wouldn't let her withdraw the tube from her pocket.

"Well, you should have thought of that before you donned the overalls, right? What if we get a scramble?"

"I don't have a Wasp now, in case you've forgotten. And I couldn't react now anyway, could I, thanks to you?"

Several napkins came flying through the air to hit him, and catcalls rang out through the galley. Some of them were funny, too, Beth had to admit.

"Well, it sucks to be you," Mercy said. "But maybe you should get back to your quarters and change, huh?"

"Should—" Beth started only to have Mercy cut her off.

"Yes, he should get going. Or don't you have the balls for it?"

"Yeah, let's see those balls," AT1 Anderson, one of the plane captains shouted out to the hoots of the others. "Are they big enough?"

"Well, are they?" Mercy asked quietly, a glint in her eyes.

Hurl stared back at her for a long moment, then shrugged. He released the neck catch, and the front opened to his naval. With the seat bonded to the bench, he wasn't graceful, but he managed to climb out and stand, stark naked, behind the bench. He performed his best 17th Century French court bow, one arm sleeping low as he bent at the waist—to the consternation of those sitting at the table behind him, then straightened up, picked up his tray, and casually walked over to deposit it on the scullery belt. Cheers, whistles, and catcalls greeted him as he looked back and nodded before disappearing down the passage.

"What was that look in your eyes, Mercy? He's a squadron mate," Beth asked as people settled back to their meals.

"Doesn't mean I can't look. Don't tell me you didn't."

Beth felt her face redden. She hadn't intended their prank to go as far as it did, but yes, she had looked when it did. Instead of answering, she walked around the table and applied the debonder, freeing Hurl's overalls. She tossed them to Badger, Hurl's roommate, telling him to get them back to him.

"Nice one," Capgun said as he passed them to take back his tray. "I give you an A-minus."

"Did we go too far?" Beth asked Mercy.

"Maybe, but what the fuck? I've got to give it to him, though. He took it well."

There was something in her voice that gave Beth pause, but she wasn't sure what it was.

"He didn't finish his meal," she said.

"I'm betting he comes back and gets another, as if nothing happened. That's what I'd do."

"Yeah, you probably would," Beth said with a soft laugh. "You have no shame."

"What's there to be ashamed about, sista?" she asked, running a hand down her side indicating her body.

"Listen up, everyone", the command master chief shouted as she strode into the galley.

"Fuck, he turned us in," Mercy said, her voice going hard. "It was a fucking prank, for God's sake."

"I've got something to tell you all. We just got confirmation. The liner *DSS Bright Voyager* was destroyed two hours ago, with 1,218 souls aboard. From all indications, it was the NSB-1's who are to blame."

Stunned silence filled the galley.

Just like that, from what had been a newbie prank that had everyone laughing, their entire purpose of being had become crystal clear.

Chapter 5

"This baby is head-and-shoulders above anything else we have," Josh said, unable to keep the gloating out of his voice as he glanced up at the VIPs.

"Is it going to keep my ass in one piece?" Beth asked.

"Well, I don't know about that. But it'll do a damned sight better."

It had been three weeks since their debrief by Doctor One Off, one week since they'd learned of the destruction of the *Bright Voyager*, and finally, they were seeing something happen. All of them had been incensed about the cruise liner and had wanted to respond, but without a specific mission, and without any modifications to their Wasps, they'd been held on the station, limited to sim battles where a new engineering liaison team was inputting different configurations for both the Wasps and NSB-1's, then sending the results back to the project head on Earth.

Beth had killed a dozen enemy fighters—and been killed 21 times herself.

Meanwhile, while VFX-99 was playing electronic games, normal line squadrons were out there escorting ships as they plied the galaxy. The cause of the destruction of the *Bright Voyager* was officially "under investigation," but with all the conspiracy theories floating about, a few were close to the truth. This couldn't be kept under wraps for long, but the Directorate wanted a solution before they broke the news, and that solution centered around the Stingers.

No one in the squadron thought the secret could be kept for long, but they dutifully kept at the simulations, hoping all those highly-paid engineers and scientists could give them the tools to fight.

It was actually amazing that in three weeks, they were already modifying the Wasps. Two mods had been approved, and the machine shop had been busy printing out the new parts. The first was the shielding, which was not simply going to be adjusted—the bells were going to be replaced to better shape the fields for the alien beam cannons. The new designs had been tested in the sims and declared more efficient.

When gushing over the *Tala*, Josh had been referring to their own hadron cannon. The synchrotron had been miniaturized, allowing for a much longer tube that ended up focusing the beam better, putting more joules on the target. Beth had watched the civilian techs replace the old synchrotron with Josh and Lieutenant Ramsey-Chord hovering like mother hens. To be honest, the new synchrotron looked pretty much like the old one to her, but both Josh and the lieutenant seemed pretty excited.

Beth was going to hold judgement until she could try the two new systems out, but she was cautiously optimistic.

VIP's from area commanders to captains and ship engineers of the larger capital ships were there as observers. There had to be 60 of them standing in a roped off area in the back of the hangar, and she understood Josh's point. Some of them couldn't keep the jealousy out of their expressions. Beth wasn't quite sure why. No one knew if the new systems would work any better against the aliens than the old. The Navy could install them now on a cruiser, for example, but if they weren't enough, a capital ship with 500 sailors would be lost. No, the brass thought it better to lose a single-seat fighter with one sailor aboard.

Beth knew the decision was the right one, but she didn't have to like it. She wanted a chance to kill the NSB-1's, not venture out under-armed and under-protected with no chance of success.

"Let's go, Fire Ant," Lieutenant Commander Vestergaard said, slurring the two words together to a "FirANT." "We've got the mission brief in five."

"I've got it," Josh said to her. "She'll be ready."

"I'm on my way, sir," she said, following Gollum out of the hangar.

There was no time to waste, and the project civilians needed real-life data to crunch. The squadron was going out to the range in three hours to test out the modifications.

Beth was sure Josh would have the *Tala* ready. The question was if the modifications were the right ones.

****

They weren't.

Eight hours later, the tractors brought the *Tala* back into the hangar. She retracted the canopy and hopped to the deck where a worried-looking Josh came running up, wringing his hands.

"Sorry about that—" he started before Beth cut him off.

"Not your fault. It's their mods," she said, nodding at the host of civilians who were being held back until all the fighters had been recovered. "They rushed through the development."

That probably wasn't fair. The onsite project head had briefed them that this was only a preliminary test and not a roll-out of combat-ready modifications, but it was easier to blame them than just chalk this up as business as usual.

The mission had not been true combat training. The drones had fired low-powered simulated NSB-1 beam cannons at them, and Beth had been "killed" twice. The only reason she hadn't been killed more times was because after her shielding had been knocked offline twice, she hadn't been able to reset and bring it back online.

The control flight, made up of three of the squadron's general frames, none of which had been modified, fared far better than the Wasps with the so-called new-and-improved shielding.

Beth had been royally pissed off when she was left without working shielding, and she'd uttered a few profanities that would have made Mercy proud. Most of that was frustration that the test had failed, and that meant it would be longer before the squadron would be ready to get back into the mix. A good part of that was because as with all of the pilots who had tested the shielding first, she hadn't been able to test her new cannon. Without shielding, even if they were in what was considered secure space, protected by six heavy monitors and a dozen stationary pillboxes, regulations required them to return to the station.

"So, what do they say?" Beth asked her plane captain.

"That it was to be expected. They said there was bound to be some glitches."

"Glitches? My friggin' shields collapsed! I was out there with nothing!"

"I know, I know. But we can install the old bells and reprogram the rest to put the old system back in for now."

"Just don't let them screw up the *Tala*, OK? I want you to watch them."

"Oh, don't worry about that. I'm on it, I swear to you."

She knew he would. Beth loved the *Tala*, she loved flying her, and she loved just being in the cockpit. Josh LOVED the *Tala* as if she were an extension of his being. Sometimes, Beth thought that he was being magnanimous by *allowing* her to fly the fighter.

Far from being annoying, Beth thought that was a valuable character trait in a plane captain. She wanted someone personally vested in their Wasp. Most of what a plane captain did was routine: running diagnostics and replacing modules if the need arose. Still, there could always be unforeseen issues that went beyond the checklists, something that could be missed by those techs who were not as vested in their jobs and Wasps.

This was particularly true when there were no approved checklists yet with the modifications. Josh may not be an engineer, and he may not understand the science of all the modules it took to keep a Wasp flying, but while the *Tala* was being tinkered with, she felt more reassured with Josh watching over her.

Over by his Wasp, the lieutenant commander was twirling a forefinger in the air. Beth wasn't a Marine, but she'd seen enough holovids to know that was some sort of sign in grunt-speak to gather around. Beth raised her hand in what was undoubtedly not a grunt-speak sign to let him know she understood.

"OK, Gollum's calling me over for the debrief. I don't know what I can tell them other than the shields failed. Let our vaunted engineer friends figure out why. But you stay here. I don't want any of them to touch the *Tala* without you watching."

VFX-99 was supposed to be the tip of the spear, ready to take the fight to the aliens. Instead, it was the other squadrons and capital ships that were out there now while the Stingers sat on their asses.

Beth wanted—no, needed—to get out there and bring the fight to the enemy. She had a personal stake in the fight. They'd killed Swordfish, they'd killed her fellow squadron mates, they'd killed the people aboard the *Bright Voyager*, and she wanted to extract revenge. That might not be healthy, and she'd never mentioned any of that to the psych programs for fear of being pulled off flight status, but it was what it was. She wanted payback.

Chapter 6

"I'm sorry it has to be like this," the commander said, handing Beth the small blue case. "We should have had a ceremony, orders be damned."

Beth had to smile. In typical GT fashion, he thought he could pretty much do what he pleased, and in most cases, he was right. But this was the Navy, a monolith that in many ways ignored the rich and powerful.

She opened the case. The medal was brilliantly burnished, as if the star was shining. The deep black ribbon, edged in platinum silver, seemed a polar opposite, as if it was sucking all the light from the room. There was some pretty high tech going on with the fabric, and Beth touched it, half-expecting her finger to disappear into it. In the middle of the ribbon was a single small propeller.

Beth had been awarded the Star of Valor First Class, referred to as the "Platinum Star" for the color of the star itself and the ribbon edging, for her actions in SG-9222. However, as the battle was still highly classified, she was not authorized to wear the ribbon on her uniform.

That didn't bother her as much as she thought it would. Someday, when the public was told of the threat, she'd be free to wear it. Until then, at least the rest of the pilots and many of the other squadron sailors knew.

Still, it would be nice to show off for the SEALs, she told herself.

The squadron shared the station with a SEAL company, and they had a somewhat condescending attitude to the squadron, as if flying a fighter wasn't "real" military. The one time she'd gone to the gym with Hurl, she'd only been able to take their "Oh, isn't she cute trying to bench 20 kilos," for ten minutes before she abandoned her fellow pilot and got out of there. No, Beth couldn't bench press a tenth of what they could, and no, she didn't know a hundred ways to kill an enemy with a strand of spaghetti or whatever those snake-eaters did, but she wondered how well any of them could fly a Wasp.

She slowly closed the case, then said, "It's OK, sir. A ceremony isn't important. I'm just honored to have been awarded it."

"You deserved it. All of you did," he said to the others in his office.

Mercy had been awarded the Star of Valor Second Class, the "Gold Star," and Warthog, Ranger, Bull, and Uncle received the Star of Valor Third Class, the "Silver Star."

None of them had mentioned Tuna and Swordfish. Tuna had been awarded the Platinum Star, posthumously, while Swordfish would be awarded the Order of Honor, also posthumously. The OOH had been approved by the Directorate and was now going through the paperwork. Neither award would be made public for now. Tuna's wife and kids were still on Charlie Station, just a short inter-system hop away, but they wouldn't know anything until all of this became public.

That rather sucked, Beth thought. Both men were dead, and their families had thought they'd died in a training accident. Swordfish had willingly sacrificed his life so that Warthog could get vital information back to the Navy, and his parents didn't know he'd died a hero.

"Well, once this is all unclassified, maybe we can do this up proper," the commander said. "But for now, this will have to do. All I know is that you made the Stingers proud.

"Command Master Chief, do you have anything to add? XO?" Both of them shook their heads, so the commander said, "Well, I guess that's it. Really, I'm sorry these had to be handed out like the Plan of the Day."

He shook Beth's hand, then did the same with the rest. The XO, and even Command Master Chief Orinoco shook each of their hands as well.

"Good job, Dalisay," the command master chief mumbled, perhaps the first positive thing she'd said to Beth since she reported in.

"I bet that hurt her to say," Mercy said as they left the commander's office and headed back to their quarters.

"Eh, she had to keep up the forms," Beth said. "I'm not too concerned what she says. I just wished she'd lay off the working parties."

It wasn't as bad as when she first reported in, especially with Hurl now in the command master chief's sights, but Orinoco was still tapping her for working parties far more than mere rotation among the junior petty officers would reflect. She'd done far worse as a domestic on Bally's World, so the work itself didn't bother her, but just the fact that she was being singled out did.

"Let me see your medal," Mercy said.

Beth stopped and opened the case.

"Mighty fancy," Mercy said.

She opened her case and held it up to Beth's. They were basically the same medal. Mercy's star was gold instead of Beth's platinum white, and the border on the ribbon was gold as well. But the black of the ribbon was the same, as was the propeller device.

Modern fighters were centuries away from propeller-driven planes, but the Navy loved tradition and history, so the props, or "egg-beaters," as they were called, were used to denote valor in fighters, scouts, reconnaissance, atmospheric planes, and other small vessels. Valor in a capital ship was designated by a fouled anchor. The Marines and SEALs had their own device, crossed swords, to designate valor on land.

Beth tapped her egg-beater with one finger, then reached over to tap Mercy's. She had no idea what prompted her to do that. It wasn't a tradition of any sort, but it just felt right. Mercy was her wingman, and they were bonded in combat.

Hopefully soon, they'd be back in combat again, and not sitting on their asses back in the station.

Chapter 7

"Satan's balls, what the hell is that?" Mercy said as they trooped into the hangar where a single Wasp was on pad 101. "It looks like a Carnival float."

Beth was speechless.

As a dual space/atmospheric fighter, a Wasp was a "clean" vessel, sleek and mean-looking. Looking mean had no actual value in combat, but the pilots were inordinately proud of their fighters' looks.

This Wasp didn't look mean. Sprouting off the stern like a peacock's tail was delicate-looking lattice frame that reached out ten or twelve meters. Like proud parents, Dr. One Off and five of her team stood in front of the Wasp as the pilots gathered round.

"Thank you for coming," the doctor said. "I believe you will be pleased with the latest upgrades to your Wasps. I've taken the lessons learned from the prior testing to develop this new prototype," she said, patting the hull of the fighter.

"I have three major and eleven minor modifications that I am confident should result in a much higher offensive lethality coefficient during NSB-1 engagements."

What? You mean we can kill more bad guys? Just say that, then.

"The initial modifications to the P-13 tested well during field trials; however, I decided to further refine the array to provide a delta of . . ."

As with every other time the doctor started off on one of her journeys into physics, Beth was lost. All she thought she picked up was that they'd improved the hadron cannon. When the subject shifted to the shielding, she perked up. This was why she'd been "killed" during the trials. Still, no matter how hard she concentrated, it might as well have been in a different language for all the good it did her. It was "better," was all she could pick up—at least that was what she hoped the doctor was saying. It wouldn't make much sense otherwise.

The doctor was beaming with pride as she went on during the brief. She kept stopping to look back at the Wasp, actually stroking it a few times. Beth wondered if she really understood that there would be pilots in them, pilots who would be taking the fight to the aliens. She didn't think so. She was getting the impression that the doctor and her team considered the Wasps as an intellectual challenge, nothing more.

"How about that medici collar," Mercy muttered when the doctor kept talking about other modifications, ignoring the elephant in the room. "You going to talk about that?"

The contraption on the stern kept drawing Beth's eyes. She couldn't imagine what it was for, and it certainly could not be intended for atmospheric flight. That meant that this Wasp was solely configured for space flight.

One of the advantages of a Wasp was that it was a very capable atmospheric fighter. It wasn't very efficient from a power-to-output-standpoint, but that was hardly a consideration given its FC engine. Wasp pilots constantly trained in using its duel capability to fight craft that were limited to one or the other. Popping out into space when fighting atmospheric planes, for example, gave a Wasp pilot far more flexibility. With that . . . *thing* attached to the back, the Wasp had just lost one of those dimensions.

It took the doctor 40 minutes before she addressed the elephant in the room, and then, it was almost as an afterthought, something that didn't adequately address her capabilities as a project head. She dismissed it as a commercially available radiator, designed to radiate heat into space. All that had to be done was for the Navy frame techs to cut it to fit and then tie it into the Wasp's ATCS. Evidently, because it hadn't taken her team to create it, it was barely worth mentioning.

With her brief over, the doctor, her team following like ducklings, filed through the pilots and out of the hangar. Captain Ostermaan, the Navy head of the project, stepped up. His presence was somewhat awkward, at least to the squadron. Commander Tuominen was their commander, and before the captain's arrival, the senior officer aboard Sierra Station. The Navy wasn't going to let a high-ranking civilian, and a GT at that, to run the show, so they sent in Captain Osterman to represent the Navy and run interference for the squadron if it became necessary.

"I realize that all of you understood every word Doctor One Off said," he said. "I know I did. Every word. Sure."

There was a rumble of laughter from the pilots and crew. Beth was relieved that it wasn't just her who'd been lost.

"But our take-away from this is that your Wasps have been improved. Not in looks, perhaps," he said, pointing to the radiators, again as the pilots laughed, "but in performance. And we're going to need that. There are indications that our services are going to be needed sooner rather than later."

The assembled sailors exchanged looks with each other, and Beth felt a sudden jolt of energy. She hadn't heard anything about alien activity since the *Bright Voyager* was lost, but there had been hints and rumors. The captain could not go into detail here in the hangar—that would have to wait until the more secure briefing room, something Beth and the rest thought was overkill. Everyone on the station knew at least part of what was up—it was rather difficult to hide it. For him to even say what he'd just done was probably against some sort of directive. But it also drove home the point that the squadron had a mission, and they'd be called upon, soon.

"We've got our one printer here on the station, but we're also getting three more printers from Charlie Station dedicated to us, as well as another tech team that will arrive within the hour," he said. "They will be working around the clock to modify the squadron's frames. I don't think I have to verbalize just what that portends."

No, you don't, sir.

Beth didn't know how many industrial printers the shipyards on Charlie Station had to service the entire sector fleet, but a typical waiting time for a part to be printed could be as long as a couple of months. To pull three of the big printers out of the normal maintenance queue to print the parts necessary to modify the squadron's Wasps was a telling course of action.

The powers that be wanted the squadron back in a combat status, and they wanted it soon.

TJ-9755

Chapter 8

"There goes Bravo," Mercy passed on the 1P. "Getting the glory while we play spectator."

Beth understood the feeling. When the new mods had been installed, the entire squadron had been ready to go, to find the enemy and take the battle to them.

It was not to be, however. Doctor One Off had assured the commander that the FX6-L's, the "Limas," were combat ready and up to the task. The Navy top command, however, was being more conservative. A rear admiral inspector general had refused to re-certify the squadron for full combat ops, demanding not only a field trial against simulated enemy, which the squadron had completed and passed, but a limited real-time engagement.

Doctor One Off had been apoplectic over the decision, taking it to the directorate itself, but in this case, the Navy held sway. The new systems had to be tested against the enemy before the Stingers were released for full combat.

It wasn't just the civilians who were upset. A Navy Rapier, with a crew of 35, had been lost to a chance encounter with what was probably a larger enemy vessel of some kind. To a person, the squadron felt guilty, that other ships were out there plying the black while the squadron formed to meet the threat was sitting doing nothing.

The fleet commanders were anxious as well, which could be expected. They couldn't very well cease operations when hundreds of thousands of commercial ships were going about their daily business, and the Directorate was not going to ground commercial activity. Economists and sociologists had long determined that a cessation of shipping would affect billions, if not trillions, of lives, and conservative estimates were that after as little as a week, millions of people would start to die on a daily basis.

So, the Navy had to fly, but none of their ships had been given upgrades to face the threat. The operational commanders wanted those upgrades, and they wanted them now. The chief of naval operations, however, had refused to authorize the cost and effort to start adapting the modifications until they passed a proof of concept.

And all of that led to this mission. The galaxy was scanned to find signs of not just an alien presence, but a small enough presence that could be used as a test case. Now that humans were learning what to look for, it became apparent that there was significant alien activity in the Perseus Arm, moderate in the Sagittarius Arm, and as of yet only sparse activity in the Orion Arm, to which almost all human activity was still limited. Humans could theoretically reach the Perseus Arm given enough computing power to set the gates, but for many reasons, not the least that there were billions of systems in the Orion Arm alone, it was easier to stay closer to home. The fact that the aliens had a presence in three galactic regions was sobering, to say the least.

After several days (and probably much debate far above the squadron, or even Navy level) a target was selected. Two, possibly three alien ships were detected at TJ-9755, a previously explored system closer in to the galactic center, but still well within human space. With nothing of value discovered in the system, it had been abandoned. Having been surveyed, however, humanity had a significant amount of data at hand, data that had been entered into each Wasp's AI.

"At least we're being spectators," Beth reminded Mercy. "Be thankful for that."

"Not the same thing. We hang back while they get the glory."

Bravo and Echo Flights were the test platforms for the mission, designated Rose Flight. With eight Wasps in Rose Flight, Doctor One Off had essentially guaranteed an easy victory. Once the efficacy of the modifications had been proven, then other Wasp squadrons could be modified and the same concepts could be used to start modifying the capital ships.

"We've got our mission, Mercy, and someone's got to do it."

"And we got it because we're fucking hobbits," she said sourly before cutting the 1P.

Beth shrugged, nonplussed. She had started her career in space because of her diminutive stature. Mass was a major concern for craft powered by the older tech—and much cheaper—Bradstone engines, the type used by commercial scouts. Smaller pilots meant smaller craft and less mass.

Mercy wasn't as small as Beth, but she was still the second-smallest pilot in the squadron. She came from a wealthy family, though, and being small had never been an advantage to her. With both of them in Fox Flight, it had been a no-brainer that if one flight was going to carry the instrumentation to gather the data needed to re-certify the squadron, it was going to be Fox. While Capgun was a fairly large man, Gollum was on the short side as well.

The four Wasps were jammed-packed with the extra equipment, both in the cockpit and carried in external pods that had taken the place of torpedoes. This was the second time the *Tala* had been used like this, and while Beth wasn't happy about it, she had been serious when she told Mercy that it was better to be a spectator than staying back on the near side of the final gate as security.

"Fox Flight, commence gate approach," Gollum passed.

There wasn't a real reason to verbalize the order—the four Wasps were on an automatic approach, but procedures were procedures, and verbal commands had probably been used since the very first gate jump.

Beth let her eyes drift to the panel at the top of her head's-up—the approach was green with a gate entry of 25 seconds. With her helmet on, she couldn't pull her cross out of her flight suit and kiss it, but habits died hard, and she mimed the action. Then, as always, she held her breath for the last five seconds, only letting the breath out once she was safely inside the TJ-9755 system.

Four of her instruments were to be turned off while passing through the gate, so her first order of business was to turn them back on. Only then could she get her bearings.

Beth had been in some amazing systems during her career as a scout pilot, with huge gas giants, ringed planets, and asteroid belts. This wasn't one of them. The system was a red dwarf with four unassuming planets at close orbit. Only one was within the Goldilocks Zone, and that was by stretching the definition of the term. That planet was a viscous caldron of gasses which were poisonous to carbon-based life. Among the gasses were traces of chlorine, which raised some interest. If, in fact, the aliens were chlorine breathers, then could they be interested in the system for habitation? Did they have an alien form of terraforming, to make the planet like their home?

If they hadn't shown themselves to be aggressive by murdering humans, Beth would have been fine with leaving the system to them. But they had attacked and killed, so, that was off the table.

Two minutes ahead of Fox, Bravo and Echo were streaking toward the planet from which the readings had been picked up. Fox started a slow wheel, coming around to facilitate a quick retreat, if necessary. Their instruments could pick up the two flights from anywhere within the system, so there wasn't a strategic reason for them to close the distance.

The XO, who was also the flight leader with Echo, was the mission commander. She had Echo and Bravo in a crossed zipper-fours, which was the space version of a finger four formation in atmospheric tactics. With her as the "middle finger," the other seven Wasps positioned on her, providing maximum fire power to the front, but allowing both flights to separate and maneuver independently should the situation demand it.

Other than turning on the four instruments, Beth didn't need to do anything with them, so she watched the XO lead her flights forward, closing the distance to the planet. There was no sign of the enemy. The methodology used to detect enemy activity was questionable at best, and Beth began to wonder if this was a dry well, something she'd become accustomed to in the past. Out of her 56 civilian scout missions for Hamdani Brothers, only five had not been dry wells: four had paid bonuses, and in the last one, she'd been attacked by the aliens.

"You getting anything?" she asked Mercy.

"Hell, I don't know how to read all this stuff. I'm just hauling it around."

Beth meant from her Wasp's normal sensors, but it had been a stupid question. If Mercy could pick something up, so could Beth. Besides, Rose Flight was quite a bit closer, and they'd most likely pick up before Fox Flight could.

"I'm just wondering if this is going to be a dry well."

"Dry well? What the hell is that?"

"You know what . . ." she started before she realized she had slipped back into scout talk. The Navy didn't use the term. "I mean, that there's nothing here."

"Nothing here with us, sure. The XO still has a long way to go. And you heard the brief. If the FALs are on the planet with all the gas soup, then they're going to have to get almost to the planet before they can pick something up."

And if they are on the planet, maybe they're just the FAL version of a scout. Not much of a test.

Without a decent nickname and NSB-1's being rather unwieldy, some in the squadron had started to refer to the aliens as "FALs," as in "fucking aliens." Mercy, of course, had immediately jumped on board that.

"I guess we'll know in an hour or so," she said, looking up at the mission timer. It was a H-plus-12, with Rose reaching the planet at around H-plus-75.

Meanwhile, Fox was just cutting a round hole in space, staying on station until the mission was completed or called off.

She pulled down her drinking tube, banging her elbow on the GTG-49 Displasia Anometer. She had no idea what the thing did, only that part of it extended into an extremely awkward position for her. Connecting the tube to her helmet nipple, she sucked in a gulp of Energy-3, wishing it was a Coke. Josh had been able to rig the *Tala* with the forbidden beverage before, but with all the engineers poring over the Wasp, Beth had put the nix to that for the duration.

The alarm caught her mid-swallow, and she spewed the liquid across her helmet faceshield.

Hell, glad it wasn't Coke.

She slaved to the XO's display. Two vessels, matching the enemy specs, had appeared near the planet and were accelerating toward Rose Flight. If the two were a simple scout mission, then they were using craft with the same specs as those that had attacked them in SC-9222.

"This is—" Mercy started before Gollum overrode her with, "Rose Flight's got contacts. Looks like the NSB-1's. Nothing has changed for us, though. Keep to the plan."

"Someone's going to get a kill," Mercy said to Beth on the 1P. "Fuck, I wish it were me."

Beth loved Mercy, and she knew Mercy loved her, but she also knew her friend was somewhat jealous of Beth's two kills. There was something in her irreverent, happy-go-lucky manner that hid a burning desire to excel past everyone else.

"Just stay steady, Mercy. Unless we find out all of this is a mistake and peace breaks out, we'll get more than enough opportunity to fight in the future. All of us will."

"Peace breaking out? Fuck that shit," Mercy said.

For the next 13 minutes, the two forces closed. The first to blink were the aliens, firing off a salvo of four of their round torpedoes. Immediately, the XO broke the zipper-four into two diverging flights, dispersing and forcing the torpedoes to choose which flight to follow.

Beth was impressed by the precision of the maneuver. They'd lost no speed, they were still closing with the enemy, but now, they presented a more dispersed front.

Echo fired first, two pilots on the new cannon. They fired in nano bursts in shotgun mode, each shot spread out so that if the oncoming ships maneuvered before the beam reached them, the theory was that they couldn't maneuver free of the spread.

The range was still long, and Beth watched breathlessly as her display illuminated the beam track as it sped through space to the enemy.

"Holy shit! They splashed one!" Mercy shouted as one of the enemy ships disintegrated.

Beth stared at the display, then shouted into her helmet. Firing at this range had been part of the process of gathering data. It had not been expected to succeed. But there was no doubt about it, one of the alien ships was no more.

"I guess the new beamer works," Capgun said dryly over the flight net as if this was routine.

"One more left," Mercy said, far more excited.

"Clear the net," Gollum passed. "Just keep on station."

Rose Flight turned its attention to the incoming torpedoes. Their improved shields would not be much good against them, so it was time to take them out before they could reach the Wasps. Three of the Wasps in each of the two flights concentrated beamer fire while tracking with their rail guns, while one Wasp in each flight dispersed wider and kept focused on the remaining alien ship.

The torpedoes were seemingly made of sterner stuff than the ship. Despite the fire control AI's cycling through various frequencies and amplitudes, the torpedoes kept coming, the enemy fighter in trace.

The range kept closing, and Beth began to get nervous. After that first easy kill, her optimism was beginning to fade. At less than 200 megaklicks, one of the torpedoes finally spun out of control. That still left one more, and it kept advancing until Echo's rail guns opened up, exploding it at 1.5 megaklicks—too close for comfort.

"Whoa! It wasn't that hard before," Mercy said.

"It looks like we're not the only ones making modifications," Beth answered.

As soon as the second torpedo was taken out, the surviving ship veered off, trying to break contact. The XO now had a judgement call to make. With eight Wasps in the two flights, and with the new cannons proven, it shouldn't be difficult to chase down and destroy the enemy fighter. However, the squadron couldn't be recertified until it had taken fire, both from the enemy beam and microwave weapons. If that didn't happen during this mission, recertification would have to wait for a subsequent mission.

"Bravo, push forward. Echo, hang back. Let's see if we can't tempt our friend into taking a few potshots at us," the XO passed.

"Playing target, the poor bastards," Mercy said to Beth on the 1P. "Gotta love it."

Beth had done it before, and she didn't envy Bravo. Fighter pilots were trained to take the fight to the enemy, not let the enemy have a free shot at them. Still, it had to be done.

Bravo-2 and 3 dialed back their cannons and fired on the alien ship. They were trying to goad the enemy to fire back while not destroying it. Beth couldn't tell if they were having any effect. The ship kept fleeing.

For the next 12 minutes, Bravo crept ever closer, peppering the enemy but drawing no fire.

"Maybe they already knocked out the FAL's weapons," Mercy passed.

"They haven't targeted it at full power," Beth reminded her.

"Well, it's just running away, so unless you have a better idea, I'm sticking with that. We might as well just splash it before it shoots its gate and gets away."

Under no circumstances were any of the Wasps authorized to go chasing an enemy ship through a gate. If the enemy ship did manage to jump out of the system, it would be safe.

One of her instruments—she didn't know which one— was scanning the system, watching for any fluctuations in emissions. No one knew exactly how the NSB-1s travelled between systems, and while testing the weapons and shielding was paramount, gathering secondary data was still vital. She thought Mercy was right about the enemy fleeing, so as Bravo closed in on the surviving enemy, she watched the alien's flight path, then projected it forward. There was no practical reason to do that, but if the enemy did enter a yet unseen gate, she wanted to see it.

The blossoms of energy sprang up like mushrooms after a storm, not in one spot, but scattered. It took a moment for Beth to realize what she'd seen. Twenty-seven ships suddenly appeared, positioned like a sack around Echo and Bravo. Rose flight was in a kill zone, and the bandits opened up.

"Tally twenty-five bandits. Rose Flight, break, break, bug now, buster to mother," the XO passed. "Fox Flight, give us some support."

"Weapons free," Gollum passed. "Make them count."

The "fleeing" enemy ship spun on its axis and fired on Park in Bravo-2. An experienced recon pilot, this was his first combat mission in a fighter. He splashed the enemy craft, and Beth whooped while she commenced her own fire. Instead of turning away, though, Park headed right for the other ships that were closing in, his cannon blazing while he launched his torpedoes.

"Break, Kimchi," the XO ordered.

"They've got lock on me," he passed. "And I'm burning up."

Oh, shit, was all Beth could think.

"Fuck! My peacock tails' gone!" he passed, his voice bordering on panic. "It's fucking gone!"

"Bug out, Kimchi!" the XO passed again.

But it was too late. Kimchi was gone, his passing marked by a tiny explosion as his self-destruct ensured there was nothing left of him or his Wasp for the enemy to analyze.

The self-destructs, which were tiny nukes, had been installed only a week before. It had been sobering when they were installed, but even more so now that the first one of them has been triggered.

"Rose Flight, firewall it. Keep up the targeting, but bug out. Gollum, head for the gate. Keep up the supporting fire, but do not hesitate. You need to get back with the data. The ATCS is not working, I repeat, not working."

"Roger that," Gollum passed, the on the flight net, "You heard the XO. RTB, but keep up the supporting fire until we pass the gate. Make sure your IFF is on. The monitor on the other side is going to be on high alert as you shoot the gate."

Beth gave the order as the *Tala* sped up to the gate. She'd be through it within ten minutes, safe and sound. She didn't think Rose Flight would. Like a giant drawstring pouch, the enemy were closing in on Bravo, and the three remaining Wasps were running.

An enemy ship was destroyed, then another, but there were just too many of them out there. This had been an ambush, pure and simple, and the flight had walked right into it.

"The ATCS is not effective," Thunder, the Bravo Flight leader passed. "The peacock tails are coming apart."

"Can you break free?" the XO asked.

"Not like this," Thunder replied, then a moment later, "Kicking G-shot."

Witchy in Bravo-4 winked out before the G-shot could take effect. Beth had kicked G-shot on GC-9222, and the extra speed had probably saved her life and certainly saved Bull's life. The recovery back on Sierra Station had sucked, but it was better than the alternative. She tried to will the avatars on the screen to move quicker, getting out of the kill zone, but just as she could see the remaining two Wasps start to accelerate, Thunder's avatar winked out.

"Fox Flight, commence gate approach," Gollum passed, his voice calm.

"This isn't right," Mercy passed on the 1P. "We're running again."

"With vital information, Mercy. And the XO ordered us out."

"But, those are our friends!"

"Who we can't help."

"We can splash those motherfuckers!" she almost snarled into her mic.

"Mercy, get ahold of yourself. We're winchester on torps and too far for the railgun. We've got the cannon, but there's twenty-two of them closing in. Follow your orders," Beth said, hoping that Mercy would listen.

Her roommate didn't say anything else, but neither did she deviate from her approach. Beth counted that as a win.

"Echo, kick G-shot," the XO passed.

G-shot enabled a pilot to endure super-high Gs that would otherwise kill them, even with the compensators maxing out. A Wasp could still fight under max acceleration, but the pilot's brain and reflexes tended to suffer. Beth was saddened, but not surprised when only three of the Echo Wasps started accelerating. The XO did not kick his G-Shot. He was going to cover the rest.

He managed to splash one more enemy ship before Beth shot the gate, IFF blaring to let the monitor know she was a friendly.

Only two Echo Wasps made it through the gate. Their "guaranteed" mission had resulted in six losses. As Beth made her round-about way back to Sierra Station, her precious instruments intact, she brooded in anger.

Someone had to pay for this.

SIERRA STATION

Chapter 9

It was an angry group that waited in the conference room. Some of the pilots were grumbling in groups while others, including Beth, brooded in silence. Her imagination was full of images of Doctor One Off roasting over a spit, of her being quartered by horses.

No, not horses. Too quick.

The squadron had lost six pilots, six friends, all because the damned radiators had been pieces of shit that hadn't worked. Rose Flight had been sent in to be targeted, and that had been their demise.

Almost all of the anger in the squadron was aimed solely on the GT. She was the one who'd taken the credit upon her shoulders, she was the one who'd promised them an easy victory. She hadn't been the one to put her ass on the line to test her great modifications, however.

Convenient, that.

Beth knew that the doctor hadn't purposefully sent Rose Flight on a suicide mission, but that didn't matter. Beth and the rest needed a focus for their anger. They needed to lay blame, and she was the obvious choice. Heck, she was probably upset as well, but not for the same reasons as the pilots. From her perspective, the failure in the radiators would be a failure in her scientific leadership.

The back hatch swung open, and as one, the seated pilots stood up and turned. Commander Tuominen, Captain Ostermaan, and two unfamiliar civilians walked into the room and made their way to the front.

The commander took the podium and said, "Please take your seats."

No one did.

"Where's that fucking GT?" Bull shouted out, ignoring the fact that the commander was one of the Golden Tribe as well as the doctor.

"Uh . . . Doctor One Off has been recalled for consultation. We just saw her and her team off before coming here."

The group erupted in protest.

"Just like that? She fucks us over, and she leaves?" CWO3 Idle shouted out.

"It wasn't her choice. As I said, she and her team were recalled. So, please, take your seats so we can start."

The pilots were on edge and angry, and they didn't want to sit down, but the commander was their CO, and discipline had been drilled into them. In fits and starts, they started to take their seats, but everyone's attention was fixated on him.

"The mission was a success—" he started before being interrupted by a massive protest.

"At ease, at ease" the command master chief, who'd been standing in the back of the room, shouted.

The commander held up a hand, and in a calm voice, said, "I know the cost was high. Too high. But that doesn't negate the fact that the mission was a success. For you to negate that is to besmirch the sacrifice of the XO and the others. Did they die for nothing? Were their lives wasted? Is that what you're trying to tell me?"

Beth had been as angry as the rest, but the commander's calmly voiced accusation hit home, and she suddenly felt guilty.

GT's were known for being able to manipulate norms—that was one of the reasons they had managed to rise in power to the point that they essentially controlled humanity. Beth knew that, and for a brief moment she wondered if this was more of that Jedi mind control stuff. But no, what he was saying made sense.

Of course, that's what I'd think if I **was** *being controlled.*

There were still some muted murmurs, but the group of pilots quieted down.

The commander closed his eyes for a moment, head tilted back, before looking out over his pilots again.

"We can't bring our brothers and sisters back, and we'll have our heroes flight tomorrow, but for now, let's examine the mission while it's still fresh in our minds."

Heroes flight? I thought . . .

They hadn't had one for Swordfish or Tuna due to the classification clamped on their mission. She wondered what had changed. Something told her that the commander might be bucking orders on this. Risky, that, even for someone with his connections, but it was the right thing to do, she thought. The six who were lost deserved that, at least.

"With that in mind, I'd like to turn this over to DO-13 Wyman, who is temporarily in charge of the Mod Team."

"Just a DO-13? What was One Off? A DE-5 or something?" Mercy asked.

"Guess there wasn't anyone that high up over at sector headquarters who could take over on short notice," Beth whispered back as Mr. Wyman took over the podium.

If he was nervous at being thrust into the position, he didn't show it. Probably in his mid-thirties with no sign of body sculpting, he exuded the confidence of someone who knew he was right.

"Thank you, Commander," he said, nodding to where the CO was sitting in his seat before turning back to the rest of the pilots. "And as he told you, this mission was a rousing success. We learned that the beam cannons were effective, and we learned that the radiators didn't work, even if that knowledge was gained at a high price. In science, proving a negative can be just as valuable as proving a positive."

"Not in the Navy. 'Proving a negative' is another way of saying you got your ass kicked," Bull called out from behind Beth.

The gathered pilots sat stock still. As a DO-13, the engineer was not that senior, holding a military equivalent to a lieutenant commander, if Beth understood the comparison correctly. Warrant officers tended to be salty, but this might be pushing decorum, and who knew how the engineer would react?

To Beth's surprise, the engineer nodded, then said, "Of course, you are correct. When it gets down to it, this is not some academic exercise. What we are trying to do is create systems to save lives. If the six of you who lost their lives on your last mission did so while obtaining the knowledge we need to create better weapons and defenses, then they will have died enabling more to live—more Navy pilots, more capital ships, more civilians. On a personal level, their deaths were tragic. On a grand scale, proving this negative, proving that the heat exchangers Doctor One Off's team developed did not work, well, that kept the same concept from being implemented Navy-wide, leaving a huge vulnerability that the NSB-1's could exploit.

"Please don't let it sound like I am belittling your compatriot's lives. Far from it. I honor them and will do my best to make sure we take the knowledge they obtained and create something that will work."

"I hate to say it, but he's right," Beth whispered to Mercy, who merely grunted.

Beth had been full of anger since the completion of the mission, and she'd been stewing in that anger, thinking fanciful thoughts of revenge. But this young engineer, who, unlike Doctor One Off, spoke on a level she could understand, had put things into perspective. Along with everyone else, she mourned the six dead, but this was always a possibility as a Wasp pilot.

She gave a quick look around the room. This fight with the NSB-1's was only going to get more involved. How many more of them were not going to survive the incipient war?

Chapter 10

"You just going to lie there like that? Our ride leaves in 50 minutes, and as they say, 'Time, tide, and formation wait for no one.' You can add shuttles to the list," Beth told her roommate.

"I'm not going on the shuttle, so I can lie here if I want," Mercy said, not looking up from her scanpad.

"Uh, I think you might have misheard. This is the only shuttle to take us to Charlie. Miss it, and you get to cool your heels here for the break."

"I didn't mishear. I'm staying right here in Sierra. It'll be nice to have some privacy," Mercy said with what sounded like a hint of bitterness in her voice.

Beth stopped her packing, a pair of shorts in her hands, and stared at her.

"I don't understand. You heard the commander. This will probably be your only chance to get home for the duration. In fact, he ordered us to leave and clear our heads."

This welcomed, if enforced leave, had come as a surprise. Activity had been frantic as Mr. Wyman—Jean-Luc, as he insisted on being called—organized his team to implement the instructions coming from what had to be a dozen labs from throughout human space. With so much input, getting a singular plan of action was difficult, and the squadron personnel hovering about, scrutinizing every single detail of what was being done to their Wasps, had to be making things even more complicated.

Commander Tuominen had zero control over what was being done to the fighters, but he could affect squadron personnel. Two hours ago, he'd called everyone into the hangar where he announced that except for a skeleton crew, every single member was to go on leave. They were to get out of Jean-Luc and his team's hair and clear their minds for what was likely to be an intense and long period of fighting.

Part of Beth recoiled at the notion, that she'd be going home to New Cebu and see her family when humanity was already in a state of war, even if very few people knew that yet.

But only part.

The rest of her was excited. Her family was very close, and she hadn't been home for six years. Whatever guilt she felt had been long washed away by enthusiasm. She'd been so happy as she got ready, telling Mercy what she was going to do as soon as she arrived, that she'd barely noticed that her roommate had not been packing.

"The CO can tell me to take leave, but he can't tell me where I need to take it. I choose to take it here," Mercy said, not looking up from whatever novaholo she was watching.

"But . . . but what about your family? Don't you want to see them? It might be years before we can get leave again."

"Fuck them. They don't care about me, and I sure the hell don't care about them. No, I'll just kick back and relax here."

Beth dropped the shorts she was holding in her hand, then sat down at the foot of Mercy's rack. She was flabbergasted and didn't know what to say. She started to speak several times, then cut off.

She'd been Mercy's roommate, her wingman, for almost five months now, and she'd never suspected that there were any problems at home. It wasn't as if Mercy didn't talk about them. Beth knew that her family was quite well-off, and she gathered that they'd had other plans for her than being in the

Navy, but there had been no hint that there was anything serious between them.

She put her hand on Mercy's leg. Her roommate tensed up but didn't jerk her leg away.

"I think maybe it would be a good idea to see them. Family is paramount."

At that, Mercy did jerk away and snarled, "You don't know what you're talking about. Yeah, I know your family is so perfect, that your hordes of sibs and cousins are just one big happy celebration of life, but not everyone is so lucky as you. Not everyone is so perfect, you know."

Where did that come from? Perfect?

Truth be told, Beth had been a little jealous of what Mercy had told her about her life. From a childhood where food wasn't a sure thing, much less the rest of the luxuries Mercy had enjoyed, her roommate's life had seemed pretty good to her.

"I . . . I don't mean that, Mercy. I didn't mean that. I mean, we're not perfect. And I just thought . . . I didn't know . . ." she said, trailing off.

She sat there in silence for a few moments, then quietly said, "The CO did say he wanted us off the station, though. To keep us out of Jean-Luc's hair."

"So, I'll fucking go to Charlie, or down to Refuge. I'm so fucking lucky to have money, right? I can check myself into one of the Sugar Range resorts. Yeah, a massage every day by some handsome stud. Just great."

Beth was lost. It was beyond her comprehension that someone wouldn't want to go home. That was where the heart resided; that was where family was. She felt a surge of pity for her friend, a friend she'd thought had everything. It didn't seem right that Mercy would be alone from everyone over the leave period that was supposed to recharge them for what was to come.

Hell, no. It's not going to happen.

She got off the rack and reached under it, pulling out a seabag that she threw at her roommate.

"Pack. Now."

"How many times do I have to tell you to get it through your thick skull that I'm not going home?"

"I know you're not. Now pack."

Mercy kicked the seabag to the deck and said, "So, why should I pack, then?"

"Because you're coming with me. To New Cebu. You're not going to sit here all alone."

Beth was sure she caught a flash of . . . interest? . . . in Mercy's eyes before she frowned and went back to her scanpad. Beth took the scanpad out her hands, turned it off, and said again, "Pack.

"Tell me, honestly, would you rather sit here in Sierra or soak in the Palawan hot springs? We've got hunky masseurs there, too, you know."

"Hmph. Now give me back my scanpad."

Beth held it high, then said, "You didn't answer my question."

Mercy shrugged.

"I'm taking that as a no. So, what good reason can you give me for not coming?"

"I don't want to interfere with your *perfect* reunion with your *perfect* family."

"We're not perfect," Beth said, then after a moment, added, "If it would make you feel better, we can visit my cousin Makisig."

"Why? He's perfect?"

"No. He's in prison. We're not all perfect, you know. Just mostly."

Mercy laughed then threw her pillow at Beth.

"So . . . ?"

"I . . . I appreciate the offer, Beth. Really, I do. But I'm serious. I don't want to interfere."

"You wouldn't be. I've told them about you, and they all want to meet—my mother, especially. Besides, you said I had hordes in my family. I need your help to ward off their assault. You're my wingman, right, and you promised never to abandon me, right?"

"Right. But, it's too late. You've got to leave now to catch the shuttle. I don't have time to pack," Mercy said, but Beth knew she'd won.

"You've got eight minutes. Throw some stuff in your seabag. Besides, you're freaking rich. Just buy new stuff. My Auntie Clarabelle's got a small shop, and she'd love to sell you a new outfit."

"Clarabelle? Seriously?"

"That's her name. Think of me just trying to help out the local economy—and Auntie Clarabelle'll probably give me a kickback, too, so you'd better come."

Beth nudged the bottom of Mercy's foot, waiting for an answer. Time was getting short, and she'd have to hurry to catch the shuttle as it was.

"If you're sure . . . ?"

"I'm sure, for God's sake. Get your ass up and grab what you can!"

"Fuck it all. I guess it can't be any worse that staying back here. OK, let's do it."

NEW CEBU

Chapter 11

"Mercy, there you are. You OK?" Beth asked. "My ina's asking where you went."

"Oh, sure. I just wanted to give you a chance to re-connect with your family for a moment. There's . . . there's a lot of them."

"And that's OK, I mean . . ."

"No, really. I'm fine. No martyr here. You just need a bit of family time."

Beth stared at her friend, trying to see if she was telling the truth, or if she had a problem with seeing a family so close. A bit of both, most likely, she realized.

On the trip to New Cebu, Mercy had opened up some, of being the rebel in the family, not willing to follow tradition and family expectations, getting in trouble with the law on more than a few occasions and having to have her uncle pull strings to keep her out of jail. Enlisting, which she did after a drunken night with friends, had been the last straw. Well, not quite. Refusing to let the family get her out of the enlistment had been the last straw.

"What's all this?" Mercy asked, pointing to all the holopics on the wall. "I thought it might be some sort of remembrance wall, but that's you, in a maid's get-up."

"These are all the extended family Off-Planet Workers. Our OPWs."

"That's a shitload of them. There's more here than my entire family on Wooster," she said.

"Well, that's what we do to survive. As you can see, there isn't much here on New Cebu. We've got to go somewhere else to make a living."

"You look cute, like some sort of fantasy-porn," Mercy said.

"Ssh! Don't let my ina hear that. There's lots of stories about OPWs getting contracts only to find out, well . . . that they aren't legit jobs as promised, if you know what I mean."

"I was only joking, Beth."

"I know, but better to keep all that kind of talk unsaid. It's a sore point for many of us."

"OK, sure. Sorry. But why the maid's outfit? You're in the Navy now."

"I was hired as a domestic, Mercy. I told you that. This was taken just before I left the planet. It's sort of a superstition, I guess. A holo of what you were when you left to make sure you come back."

"But you're back, so you can change it now?"

"Yeah, I guess."

"Good, 'cause you're a Navy pilot now, and that's what should be up on the wall here."

"OK. I'll mention it to Lovely. She's kinda the keeper of the wall."

"That's someone's name? 'Lovely?'"

"My cousin."

"Everyone's your cousin here," Mercy said with just a hint of wistfulness in her voice.

"Yeah, pretty much so. Anyway, the food's about ready, so, you hungry?"

"Satan's balls yeah. It sure smells good, so lead on."

"I told you, right? That the main dish is a whole pig, right? I mean the pig, tail to snout. Not fabricated meat."

"Yeah, so what?"

"Well, lots of people, especially, uh—"

"Especially rich bastards?"

"Well, yeah, they can't stomach the idea of eating a real animal."

"Don't you worry your pretty little head about that, sista. It smells great, and if it was good enough for our ancestors, let me at it."

Beth took Mercy's arm and led her through the house and outside where tables were set up under the acacia that gave the only shade in the village square. The original Cebu might be lush paradise, but New Cebu was dry and barren, and the old acacia, planted when the first Filipino settlers arrived, was a focal point of the village. About 50 friends and family had gathered to welcome Beth back. The pig, a treasure of crispy gold, took up the center of the main table—called lechon, it was usually the center dish of a festival. Her ina had bought it—with some of the money Beth sent home—and had been slowly cooking it for a day, but the rest of the dishes were provided by the others. She ran her eyes over the table, listing what she saw as her stomach growled: she spotted pancit, chicken adobo, lumpia shanghai and lumpia bituin, crispy pata, liempo, kaldereta, mechado, deep-brown longgaisa, fish sinigang, simmered afritada, kare-kare, and too many more dishes to mention. Her Uncle Rizal, remembering Beth's love of fresh bangus, had brought a plate of the fried fish. Most of all, Beth was happy to see a dish of her favorite: sisig. She missed the sour dish made from pork cheeks more than anything else.

She almost dislocated Mercy's shoulder as she dragged her friend forward to the tables.

"Hey everyone, this is my friend Mercy Hamlin. We call her Red Devil, and I want all of you to give her a Filipino welcome!"

Cheers greeted her, and Beth was sure she saw Mercy—sarcastic, irreverent Mercy—blush red. They took seats on either side of Beth's ina while the barangay president stood up welcome Beth back, then her Uncle Frank, and finally her ina stood up.

"I am so happy to have my Floribeth back home, even for just a short time. I'm so proud of her. Imagine, she left here to become a maid, and now, she's a Navy pilot. Oh, nothing against maids," she said, sweeping her hand to include the gathered people.

Many of them had done their 20 or 30 years as OPW maids before coming back home.

"I . . . I just don't have anything more to say. I'm at a loss for words."

"That's a first, Perlita!" one of the aunties shouted to the laughter of the rest.

"Well . . . um . . ."

"Let's eat, then!" Rocky, one of Beth's younger brothers, shouted out.

Beth's mother smiled and shrugged, and the village priest, someone new to Beth and who looked like he wasn't even old enough to enter the seminary, stood to give the blessing.

And then it was time to eat. As the guest of honor, Beth had to wait for the first piece of lechon, carved from the side of the pig. She took a bite, the firm white meat set off by a piece of the crackling, and everyone applauded. Then, like a swarm of locusts, the rest descended on the table. Mercy looked surprised, but Rocky took care of her, pointing out the dishes as he heaped them on her plate.

Beth looked around. She'd been to 59 systems in total, far more than most people could ever hope to visit. But here, surrounded by her family and friends, breaking bread with them, well, there really was no place like home.

Chapter 12

"Where's your mind at, Floribeth?"

"Oh, nowhere, Nanay" she told her ina, folding the shirt as she helped her mother with the laundry.

It had been somewhere, though: back at Sierra Station. Here at home, she felt cut off from the universe. Oh, she had all the news feeds, of course, but what was happening with the NSB-1's was classified. Back on Sierra Station, she knew that Jean-Luc's team would be scrambling to modify the Wasps, and only then, once the concepts were proven, would the vast task of modifying the entire fleet commence. The balance of the future could be riding on what was happening at the station, and here she was, folding laundry with her mother.

She felt guilty. She was happy to be with her family, to catch up with the little ones she'd never met, and to reconnect with her home. She had a job, however, and she wasn't doing it.

And, as much as she hated to admit it, she was bored. Not bored of her family, but the village ran at a slow pace. Nothing much happened except for gossip. That seemed to be the lifeblood of those who were still there, either back from their OPW stints or waiting to go on one.

"Are you happy, Nanay?" she blurted out.

"Happy?"

"Yes. I mean, are you happy here in San Miguel?"

"I'm as happy as anyone. As much as I can be, I guess."

"But . . . with five of us gone all the time, and Rocky next—"

"Not Rocky."

Beth knew that no one wanted Rocky to go off-planet. He was already 19, past the age when many took their first contract, but her younger brother was a gentle soul, and the general consensus was that he wasn't strong enough to survive life as an OPW. With the better salary Beth was now earning in the Navy, he didn't have to go.

"Yes, not Rocky. But with the rest of us. You're here in this house . . ." she said, trailing off.

A cloud came over her mother's eyes, and Beth immediately regretted saying that.

Beth's ina had one of the nicer houses in the barangay—paid for with blood money. Beth's father had worked 20 years as an OPW, but after seven kids, he thought he needed another contract to provide for his family. Beth had been eight and her mother was pregnant with Rocky when he left. Five months later, he was killed on a construction site. The company had paid the mandated death benefit, with which Beth's mother had bought the house and the small store in the center of the village, and had put away a small investment for Rocky's schooling.

Beth had watched her mother cry when her three older siblings had left, and Macriz, the next in line after Beth, had told her she'd done the same when she'd left on her contract. She blamed the life of an OPW for taking the love of her life, but she relied on her children to help support the extended family here on new Cebu.

"Speaking of Rocky, isn't it about time he was back?" she asked anxious to change the subject.

Her mother looked at her wrist-screen, then said, "They're on their way."

When Mercy had asked her about the hot springs she'd mentioned back on Sierra Station, Rocky had immediately offered to take her to them. Beth had said he didn't need to, but he insisted, and as he said, his jetbike could only hold two.

Mercy had oohed and aahed over the Kawasaki 90. The bike might be impressive for little San Miguel, but it was nothing compared to the big Westoff she'd had before enlisting, not to mention her Wasp, but Rocky had eaten it up. Beth didn't have the heart to shut him down, so she'd bowed out of the way, reminding herself to thank Mercy for giving her little brother a boost.

Ten minutes later, with a whine of jets, the two came back into the yard. Beth had just taken the last pair of pants off the line, so she folded them and walked over.

"Why thank you, good sir, for a lovely time," Mercy said with a courtly accent.

Rocky bowed low, one foot in front, his left hand sweeping back as he took her hand in his right and brought it up to his lips and kissed it, saying in his version of a court accent, "It is my utmost pleasure to be of service to you, m'lady." Then his voice changed to something much different, and he added, "Any service at all, m'lady, if you know what I mean."

"Rocky!" Beth shouted, shocked. "Mind your manners!"

"Oh, hi Ate," he said, a smile on his face, completely ignoring her admonition. "Did you have some good one-on-one time with Nanay?"

"Uh . . . yes, I did. But you—"

"I need to run," he said, interrupting before turning and bowing once more to Mercy. "Adieu, adieu, I bid ye adieu, until the next time, my sweet flower."

He jumped back on his jetbike, and with another flourish, he sped out of the yard.

"Sorry about that, Mercy. He's well . . ."

"Don't worry about it. I enjoyed myself, and your brother was the perfect host."

"I mean, well, he's got a few social issues, you know."

"Don't we all. We're fucking Navy pilots, sista, with lots of *anti*-social issues. He was fun. Easy on the eyes, too."

"What? Rocky?"

"Yeah, who else did you think I was talking about?"

"But he's my little brother!"

"Not so little, if you know what I mean," she said with a leering smile.

"I . . . he . . ."

"Oh, give me a break. Surely you can see what a hottie he is. I know he's your little brother, but believe me, he's packing."

"You saw?"

"It was a hot spring, Beth. What, you expected us just to look? No, we had a soak."

"You didn't—"

"Don't get your panties in a twist. No, we didn't fuck," she said, rolling her eyes. "Not that I didn't consider it. Fine tight ass, a sixpack, and well—"

"I don't want to know," Beth said, holding out her hand, palm up, as if that could stop Mercy if she was on a roll.

"Look, I know you're screwing with me, but listen. Rocky's, well, he doesn't always understand when others are joking. He has a hard time discerning others' emotions and such. I mean, he's got a heart of gold, but that means it's easy for him to be hurt. So, please, take it easy with him, OK? He won't understand when you're screwing around."

Mercy stepped up hugged Beth, saying, "Don't worry. I'm not going to hurt anyone.

"So, do you want to see our photos at the hot springs? See what a hunk your brother has become?" she asked.

"Just joking, sista, just joking," she said as Beth punched her in the upper arm. "Sides, I don't want to jeopardize you and me, you know, for when we become real sisters-in-law."

Beth rolled her eyes and said, "I don't know why I put up with you sometimes."

"'Cause you love me, that's why," Mercy said, pulling her in so she could kiss her cheek. "Now, what's for dinner?"

****

"Where are they?" Beth asked for the 20th time.

"Relax. They'll be back."

"You don't know Mercy, Nanay. She's . . . she likes boys."

"Of course, she likes boys. Many girls do."

"I mean—"

"I know what you mean, Floribeth. I'm not stupid."

"Sorry, Nanay. It's just Rocky is Rocky. I don't want him hurt. He's liable to get the wrong impression." When her ina said nothing, "Aren't you worried?"

"Of course, I'm worried," her ina snapped. "I worry every day, just like I worry about you every day. But I couldn't stop you from leaving, and I can't put him in leg irons. If he gets hurt, he gets hurt. That's part of growing up."

Beth stared at her mother in shock, then a wave of guilt swept over her. Her mother had gone through so much in life, and now here she waltzes in for the first time in six years and starts lecturing her?

"I'm sorry, Nanay. That was out of line. I'm just worried about Rocky."

"And Mercy?"

"For all her money, she's pretty messed up in some ways, but she's got a good heart."

"She wouldn't be your friend if she didn't," her mother said. "She's had a hole in her life, I can see, a hole you've been filling."

"Maybe. But I asked her not to screw with Rocky. I can't believe she did this."

"It was Rocky who asked her, Floribeth."

"She could have said no."

"And hurt him then?"

"Better a small hurt now than a big hurt later."

Five of the barangay kids came into the yard, asking Beth for a story about being in the Navy. She hadn't realized that she was something of a hero to the barangay, someone who left and made good. When Beth was a young girl, one of the men came back for a visit, bearing gifts. He'd married a wealthy woman while on his contract, and he'd seemed almost godlike to the young Beth. He'd never come back again, however, forgetting his roots. Now, Beth was the one to whom the kids looked up, and she vowed never to forget that.

She regaled them with tales, skirting the truth. A perverse part of her wanted to tell them about her Platinum Star, but she held off. They wouldn't know what that signified, anyway. Just the fact that she was a Wasp pilot was more than enough for her.

She'd become so engrossed with the kids that she'd almost forgotten about Rocky and Mercy until the two pulled up on his jetbike, Mercy sitting behind him, arms clasped around his waist. They got off and slowly turned to each other. Rocky gave her a long, hard kiss, while the kids giggled.

"That's enough for now," Beth told the kids through clenched teeth, noting Rocky's hands on Mercy's butt. "Go run home now, OK?"

"But you haven't finished the story," Grace Marie said.

"I will tomorrow. I need to talk to Miz Hamlin now."

"Floribeth," her ina said warningly as the kids ran off.

Mercy's hands lowered, and she squeezed his ass as well before breaking the hold. Rocky waved to Beth and their ina, a huge smile on his face, before getting back on his jetbike and riding off, but not before leaning over for one last kiss.

Beth strode over to Mercy, who watched Rocky drive off.

"You, come with me," she said before walking down the path between her ina's house and the neighbors.

She reached the rockpile, stopped, and turned, saying nothing as Mercy followed.

"I know what you're going to say, Beth, but I didn't plan anything. It just happened."

"You promised me," Beth said, fuming.

"No, I didn't."

"The hell you didn't. I was there, in case you forgot."

"No, I didn't forget, and no, that's not what I said. I said I wouldn't hurt Rocky."

"And yet, you go out and play with him."

"He didn't seem to have any complaints," Mercy said in her usual irreverent manner.

Beth took a step forward, her hands balling into fists. Mercy made a show of looking at her fists, then lifted her upper lip in disdain.

"Look, sista," she said, poking Beth in the chest with one finger. "I didn't plan on anything. It just happened. And you know what? I'm glad."

"Yeah, of course you're glad. Your glad when any asshole on the street slips you his cock. I guess since you never got love from your family, then you think a cock is the only substitute. Only it isn't, is it? So, you go looking for the next one."

Mercy's face went white, and her eyes went round.

Beth knew that was a low blow, but she didn't care. Family came first.

Mercy's mouth gaped open like a fish on the bank before she gathered herself.

"Oh, yes. The perfect family. Well, maybe you'd better talk to your brother sometime to see if he thinks you're all so perfect. Your perfect mother who smothers him, who won't let him do anything for himself. Then you come home, the Navy hero, and you smother him. Oh, yes, he puts on a show for you, all smiles, but what does he really think?"

"He thinks I'm protecting him from the likes of you, who'll use him and discard him, breaking his heart."

That was a stupid retort, she knew, but she didn't have anything better. Deep in her heart, she knew Mercy was telling the truth, and it hurt her deeply that Rocky had opened up to her, a stranger, and not his own sister.

"Well, even he doesn't realize it yet, I am protecting him from you. Better pull the scab now than suffer when you return to Sierra Station and forget him. 'Use them and lose them,' sound familiar? That's your modus operandi, isn't it?"

Mercy face went slack, her eyes dull, and she said, "I thought you understood me. I guess it's no surprise that once again, I was wrong."

She turned and stalked off, not saying another word.

Beth had words, though, lots of words. It took a supreme effort not to chase after her and say them. But she knew that would be a mistake. She had to let both of them cool off before something drastic was said, something from which they'd never recover.

She sat down on the rock pile, contemplating what she'd heard. Was she really being too restrictive on Rocky? She'd always protected him, but she'd been gone for six years. She wasn't about to forgive Mercy so easily, but that didn't mean her roommate had been completely wrong.

Night took over the sky, and the sounds of the barangay reached her, the sounds of love, hate, passion, and fighting— the sounds of life. She was off on her grand adventure, but this was the real galaxy. The barangay, and all the villages and cities scattered across the stars were worth fighting for, to keep them safe from the NSB-1 threat.

With a sigh, she finally stood up and started walking back, rehearsing what she was going to say to Mercy. She'd apologize for the comment about her seeking but never finding love, and then she'd explain Rocky's situation. Mercy was smart, and she'd understand why her little brother had to be protected.

She walked into the living room where her mother and Auntie Clarabelle were sitting close, talking softly. Beth nodded and headed for the hallway to the bedrooms.

"If you're looking for Mercy, she's not here," her mother said.

"Where is she?" Beth asked.

"I think you know."

"I don't have a clue."

Her auntie placed a hand on her sister's arm and said, "She thanked us for our hospitality and left with Rocky. He came and picked her up 15 minutes ago."

All thoughts of rational discussion fled, and she wheeled to go find the two.

"Stop, Floribeth! Haven't you said enough?" her mother said.

"Honey, wait until morning. Things will look better then," her auntie said

"But, I need to stop them."

"Stop them from what? They're adults," her auntie told her. "Just wait until morning, and we'll take it from there."

Beth's mind was awhirl. She didn't know what to do, but rational Beth agreed with her auntie, even if irrational Beth wanted to take action now.

She took five deep breaths, calming herself, then she nodded her agreement.

Tomorrow, after tempers cooled, would be much better. She'd go with her mother and auntie and discuss the matter like adults.

Only, she never got the chance. At 2:31 AM that morning, the recall came. Progress on their Wasps had been quicker than expected, and their leave had been cut short. She and Mercy were to be on the 6:00 AM shuttle to the spaceport to catch a military hop back to Charlie Station.

SIERRA STATION

Chapter 13

"Where's your twin?" Capgun asked as Beth slid into the seat beside him.

Beth shrugged but said nothing.

"Uh-oh. Trouble in paradise?" he asked.

"Nothing to speak of."

He turned his entire body to look at her, and suddenly serious, he asked, "Anything I need to bring up Gollum?"

"No, we're fine. No problem."

And she and Mercy were fine . . . she hoped.

After grabbing her bags, she had gone to Rocky's tiny loft over their ina's store, but he told her that she'd already left. He seemed sad, but not angry at her, so Mercy must not have said anything about their blowup. Beth had wanted to ask him what he thought of Mercy, but she chickened out. Rocky had given her a hug, and she left for the shuttleport where she sat two rows away from Mercy until they boarded. Neither had spoken a word to each other until they arrived on Charlie Station where Mercy had simply said that they had to be professional while on the job.

Beth had hoped for more, and she wished she could turn back the clock, but she'd nodded and agreed. Mercy never showed up in the quarters that evening. Beth had no idea where she'd crashed, nor did she ask.

Capgun gave her a long stare as if trying to dive deep into her mind, but he ended up nodding, then saying, "OK, but if there's anything more, you need to tell me, and we need to tell the flight leader. I don't have to remind you that we need to be a team, and I'm guessing we'll be out there again soon."

He was probably right in that, she knew. Rumors were already flying, but Beth didn't put much credence to any of them. With only five people still on their way back from leave, the commander had called for a briefing, so it was better just to wait and hear what he was about to say.

She didn't have to wait long. Within five minutes, the CO and Jean-Luc arrived.

"Wyman's still here?" Capgun asked. "I thought he was only temporary."

"Evidently, not so temporary," Beth answered.

She was surprised as well. The engineer had been pulled from Charlie Station after One Off had been shit-canned, but only because he was the senior qualified and available person around. Beth had been sure a more senior permanent on-site project head would have arrived while the squadron was on leave.

"I'm sorry to cut your leave short," the commander said without preamble. "The situation has changed, and time does not seem to be a luxury we can afford.

"On the enemy front, we are getting more indications that the NSB-1's are stirring. More pertinent, we lost an observatory in Sector Papa-Delta. We have no firm proof at the moment, but we believe that it was the enemy. The gate was immediately destroyed as per current SOP, but a microdrone is being readied to launch to see what it can pick up."

Beth knew next to nothing about the observatories scattered throughout the Orion Arm of the galaxy. She wasn't sure how many people manned each one. There had been two in *A View of Love*, the corny romcom from a few years back, but the holovids were not noted for their accuracy. Whether there had been two or a hundred in the observatory didn't matter, however.

Matters to their families, though.

From a strategic standpoint, what mattered was that the enemy was pushing forward, and they didn't have friendly intentions. If they were pressing into human space, then time for a concerted reaction was fleeting.

The commander updated them on the NSB-1s, which wasn't much. There was some conjecture as to their intentions, but still, they knew next to nothing about them as beings. They were probably human-sized based on the fighters encountered so far, and they were probably chlorine-breathers. This was about the sum total of their knowledge, and even that was conjecture.

This was beyond weird. How could they fight an enemy who was a mystery?

The commander passed the brief over to Jean-Luc. This was something into which they could sink their teeth. Pilots and techs alike leaned forward to hear what was being done to their Wasps. Beth had tried to check in immediately after returning the day before, but the hangar had been off-limits.

"Welcome back. I hope you're ready, because you'll be taking them out for validation in a little less than eight hours."

"Damned right we're ready," someone said from behind Beth.

"You'll be individually briefed at your fighter, but let me go over the basics . . ."

Over the next 30 minutes, Jean-Luc explained the mods made to the cannons, the shielding, and the heat exchangers. The cannons had proven effective, even if their efficiency had suffered once the platform was taken under fire from the enemy's heat weapon. There had been some rerouting of the ammonia cooling tubes, but that was about it for the cannons. The modifications to the shielding were completely beyond Beth's comprehension. Her take-away was that they'd be more effective, and she had to trust Jean-Luc on that.

What was completely different was the system for countering the heat weapons. Gone were the ridiculous-looking peacock tails, to her relief. Even if they had worked, they would have precluded a Wasp from entering an atmosphere.

The new system was elegant in concept—Beth had to hope it was effective. The beta version of the system essentially transferred heat-buildup to dense slugs, then ejected them out of the vessel. At some point, if the concept was validated, this would change to using the superheated slugs as a weapon, but for now, it was just a crude heat-exchanger.

The concept was so simple that the printers and machine shop had been able to quickly construct the module, replacing the rail gun for the testing phase. Beth didn't like that—the railgun had provided her with one of her two kills, after all. Jean-Luc had promised that the switch-out was only temporary. They were working on the design to incorporate both systems.

Beth was cautiously optimistic about the mods—then again, she'd thought the last mods would have worked, too, and she knew how that had panned out. All she could do was to do her part in the upcoming mission and hope for the best.

****

"Fox Flight, we have four bandits at twenty megs, four-o'clock low. Uploading now," ops passed.

"Hold steady," Gollum passed over the flight net as the images appeared on their displays. "Come to course two-two-one, zero-three-nine, zero-three-three, dispersion point-three meg, on me."

Beth brought the *Tala* into position off the flight leader's port side. She instinctively brought up the torpedo status before wiping it. There weren't going to be any torps on this mission.

"Fire Ant, you're off," Mercy passed on the 1P. "Tighten it up."

Beth rolled her eyes. She was barely out of position, less than a tenth of a megaklick, not even a thousand klicks. Mercy was just using the opportunity to remind her of their new relationship.

If she wanted to be that way, fine, but during a mission was not the time to be petty. Still, Beth eased the *Tala* into a better position.

Phase One on the firing range had gone well—not that anyone had expected anything different. The hadron cannons had not been modified, after all, only the cooling system beefed up. The flight had made their firing pass without an issue.

Beth had no idea how well Phase Two had gone. The flight had taken its turn flying through the gauntlet taking fire beamer fire. How effective the shielding was could only be determined by the data readouts.

Phase Three was going to be the main test. The Red Flight fighters had been outfitted with commercial microwaves that had been modified to simulate the enemy heat cannons. Fox Flight was going to bear the best the Red Flight pilots could throw at them, then engage with their own beamers. There was nothing with regards to tactics—this was knights jousting on horseback, hoping that their own armor and lances held up better than their opponents.

"I have Fox Flight beam cannons in T-mode. Check and confirm," the flight leader passed.

Beth checked the setting. It wouldn't serve the Navy well if the flight fired on Red Flight in combat mode. Normally, the Navy didn't like to mix live fire with training fire on the same exercise, but time was of an essence.

"Confirm T-mode," she reported, eyes on the blips on her display that indicated the bandits in front of her.

The Red Flight was in a simple box formation, oriented on Fox Flight's approach. Fox was going to go right up their gut in a text-book-perfect kill zone.

The NSB-1's started firing their heat cannons at close range, about 10 megaklicks, but whatever the engineers had rigged up for Red Flight didn't even have that range. The two flights closed in to seven megaklicks before the opposing force pilots opened up.

Beth's display flashed red along the edges, a somewhat obvious touch to differ from the normal yellow lights used for a beam hit. Another table popped up, this time with heat readings for various parts of the *Tala*. They immediately spiked, which in turn, started the ammonia flowing at a much higher pressure. As the pressurized ammonia picked up the heat, it carried it to a simple heat exchanger where the heat was transferred to molypendium billets. Molypendium was a synthetic metal, not found in nature, that had not only a very high melt temperature, but absorbed heat rapidly. Extremely dense, they'd have a huge impact on a Wasp's aerodynamics in an atmosphere, but their mass was manageable in zero-G.

Heating the molypendium into a molten state would enable them to eject more heat, but that had two major problems. The first was that would entail a different mechanism for ejecting the molten metal instead of a simple modification of their existing railgun. The second was that while the heat exchangers were fairly efficient in raising the temperature of the billets to 1100 C, the process became less efficient as the temperature climbed. With the power exhibited by the enemy fighters, trying to increase the temperature of the billets much higher wouldn't let them keep up with the enemy who could raise the temps faster than the pilots could bleed them.

"This is it," Gollum passed. "Watch the numbers. If you hit eight-zero and your automatics haven't kicked in, abort the mission."

When the moly billets, already being called fireturds by the plane techs, reached 1100 C, they should automatically be ejected. If the system failed and any Wasp reached 80% to failure, the exercise was over. Beth watched her system warning as the Wasp heated up, bathed in X-rays. When the *Tala* crossed the 50% threshold, she started getting a little nervous, and the sweat forming on her was not just because of the rising temperature inside the cockpit. At 54%, the first of the billets reached 1100 C, and the ejection system kicked in.

It was impossible for the naked eye to see a railgun round fire downrange, but the gun mechanism had been de-tuned to handle the screaming hot billets, and Beth could see the flash of light as the billets were shot off, a streak of white that quickly faded away.

"Cool," she muttered before looking back at her display.

Her temps were falling slightly. They weren't good by any stretch of the imagination, but they weren't rising anymore.

"Weapons free," the flight leader passed.

Each of them had already been designated a target, so Beth released her weapons AI, and a moment later, her beam cannon fired. Beth and Capgun were in single shot mode, maximum power every five seconds, while Gollum and Mercy were in nano-burst mode. Even more so than during Phase 1 of the exercise, Beth didn't have a clue as to how effective her cannons were. That was a matter for the mod team to determine.

They blasted through the kill zone, and the barrage ceased. The superheated billets kept ejecting for a few moments more as the temps kept falling.

"I'm getting solid reads here," Gollum passed. "Any issues that I'm not seeing. Confirm your negatives."

"Negative. No issues," Beth passed.

"Roger that. No issues with anyone. Well, let's RTB and find out how our rides did."

Hopefully, we did OK.

The situation was pressing, and the Navy couldn't hold back the fleet forever. Ready or not, this was probably what they'd be taking into combat when that inevitable mission came.

Chapter 14

"Well, that's that," Hurl said. "We're combat ready. So, when do you think we'll get a mission?" he asked Beth and NSP1 Lydia "Dewdrop" Portnoy.

"Could be in five minutes," Dewdrop said.

"Really? You think so?" he asked excitedly.

Dewdrop rolled her eyes, clapped him on the shoulder, and said, "Calm down Hurl. We'll get the mission when we get it. It isn't like the—"

"Ahem," Beth said, clearing her throat and interrupting her, then tilting her head at two of the Red Force pilots who were talking a few seats down.

"It isn't like we've got an actual enemy at the moment. No rebellions, no pirates," Dewdrop corrected herself.

It seemed strange, holding back information from the Red Force pilots, who were some of the best pilots in the Navy. Yet, those were their orders. They were used to keeping quiet in the passages and spaces, but here in the conference room, which was secure, they'd gotten used to being a little freer with their discussions.

With the Red Force flights attending the after-action report, Dewdrop had almost slipped up. Nothing in the report had made mention of the NSB-1's—it had focused on pure numbers. As far as Beth knew, none of the Red Force personnel knew just what the threat was. It had to break sometime, and soon, but that wasn't up to any of them to let something slip. The command would pass the word when they deemed fit.

The given excuse for the mission, as well as the Stinger's existence, was that they were an R&D squadron, developing new tactics and weapons. That was true enough. The little fact that they were forced to because of contact with an alien race had been conveniently left unmentioned.

At least the squadron was being certified again. The fireturds worked. One of Jean-Luc's team put the numbers up, showing how much heat was dissipated, but once again, all Beth cared about was the bottom line. Would they keep the *Tala* flying? According to the engineer, a qualified yes. Given the power of the microwaves used in the test, they would keep a Wasp operational for as long as the billets lasted.

The questions about the shielding were not answered with as much certainty. The indications were that the new mods made it more effective, but to what degree was somewhat of a crapshoot.

The last part of the test was the mods to the beam cannons. The improved cooling certainly helped, but so many factors affected a cannon's efficiency that it would be difficult to ascertain exactly how much the mods affected the weapons.

All told, Beth could live with the new *Tala*. Nothing could be developed that a determined and resourceful enemy couldn't defeat, and being a Navy pilot was inherently risky even in the best of times. Beth thought that Jean-Luc and his team had given them a fighting chance at success.

It wasn't just Jean-Luc, however. Numerous teams and labs throughout human space had contributed to the effort, most probably not knowing just what they were doing. But it had been Jean-Luc's team that had integrated all the input, printed and machined all the new parts, installed them, and upgraded the software. It had been an amazing accomplishment, especially given the short timeframe.

"Well, I'm going to chow. Are you coming?" Hurl asked.

"Lead on," Dewdrop said. "I skipped lunch, stupid me, and I'm starving."

The three left the conference room, then Beth said "I'll meet you there," before slipping into the head. She popped out a few minutes later and headed down the passage towards the galley.

"Hey, Fire Ant, right?" a voice called from behind her. "Wait up a second."

She turned to see a Red Force lieutenant hurrying to catch up. With dirty blonde hair, his green eyes caught her attention, and she wondered if they were a mod. Pilots generally weren't the type to have sculpting done, and certainly not to their eyes. A mod rejection and they'd be off flight status.

"Can I help you, sir?"

Normal military courtesies were rather lax in the squadron, with call signs being the most common form of address. That was within the squadron, though. This lieutenant was from another squadron, so he was a "sir" to her.

"Dimitri Greenbaum," he said, holding out his hand. "They call me Cossack."

"Yes, sir. How can I help you?"

"I was just . . . we were just . . ." he started, then stopped. "I just got my orders last week. I'm leaving the Red Force and heading here. Six of us are, in fact."

Beth didn't think they'd be transferring anyone out of the Stingers at this stage of the game, and she hadn't heard of any plans to expand the squadron, but it made sense. She harbored no illusions on what the future was going to hold, and they'd be losing pilots in combat. Fifty-eight Wasps were not enough to hold back the tide and were never intended to do so.

Still, this was an interesting bit of intel that the others would like to hear.

"That's great, sir. The Stingers are a good squadron. I'm sure you'll like it here."

"That's just the thing, Fire Ant. What are we getting into?"

"Sir?"

"Look. We've been sending flights up against you guys for some time now, highest priority and all. At first, we didn't think anything of it. You're a new squadron, one that has the eyes of the brass and all. And there was nothing new about the missions.

"But now, they hook us up with commercial microwave projectors? What's with that?"

Beth wanted to bug out, break contact. This was getting into dangerous ground.

"Sir, you know we're VFX-99. That's R&D. Who knows what the eggheads think of to try next?" she asked, forcing a smile on her face.

"Yeah, but microwaves? No one uses anything related to that as a weapon. We certainly couldn't fight with what they had us use in the exercise. I can think of twenty ways off the top of my head why they wouldn't work, and I can't imagine the Liberty League or the Bones coming up with something like that."

Neither could Beth. The Liberty League were pie-in-the-sky radicals who thought the Directorate the root of all evil, but they simply didn't have the resources to develop a microwave weapons system. As far at the Bones? They were pirates, nothing more, relying on cruelty and ruthlessness rather than high technology.

But while minor threats, they, and the other sideshows of humanity, were not the reason for the Stingers. And she couldn't say anything about them.

He'll know soon enough . . . if he really is coming, she thought, suddenly concerned.

It wasn't above DOI to test security within the squadron. She didn't know who this man was, or even if he was a pilot. He could be DOI, pushing to see if she would leak.

Panic almost overcame her, and she stammered out, "I don't know, sir. We just do what they tell us. If that's all, I've got a very important meeting right now, and I'm late."

Dumb! Can't you do better than that, Floribeth?

"But—"

"Sorry, sir," she said, wheeling about and walking away, dreading hearing him follow.

She made it to Echo Corridor and took a left, then immediately entered the head there. She stood by the door, ear pressed against it, listening for footsteps. She almost jumped when she heard them, but then muffled voices reached her and the steps receded.

Her heart was beating like a hummingbird's in her chest, and she fought to calm her breathing.

Come on, Floribeth. Get ahold of yourself. You don't know he was DOI, and even if he was, you didn't say anything.

She had to tell herself that several times before she began to believe it. As an OPW, she had the built-in wariness around corporate security, and she'd brought some of that baggage with her here to the squadron.

Finally, she had to laugh at herself, breaking out into giggles. This was a secure Navy base, not the set of some spy thriller. She'd overreacted, nothing more.

Still, she cracked the hatch open a sliver and looked down the passage before she slipped out. She forced herself not to look over her shoulder as she made her way to the galley.

"That must have been some shit, Fire Ant," Dewdrop said as she joined them with her meal. "I thought you must have fallen into the can."

"Hey, want some scuttlebutt?" Beth asked, ignoring her.

Asking someone if they wanted to hear some scuttlebutt was like asking a cat if it liked catnip. Six or seven sets of heads leaned in to hear, even Mercy's, who was sitting at the next table.

"Well, six of the Red Force pilots have got orders to join us."

"What? Are they getting rid of us NEP's?" Hurl asked, sounding worried.

"No, why do you ask that?" Beth asked.

"You know, Red Force are all officers."

"Relax, Hurl. They're not going to get rid of us," Dewdrop said. "It wouldn't make any sense."

"So, the Navy always makes sense?" Hurl asked.

Dewdrop ignored the question and asked Beth, "So, how did you come to this little bit of gouge?"

"One of the pilots, he told me."

"So, you're hobnobbing with Red Force pilots now? Like Hurl here said, they only take officers." She turned to Hurl and added, "And you, you're with the Stingers for the duration, and like all of us, you'll be lucky to make it through this shit alive."

Beth caught Mercy's eyes when Dewdrop said that, and her ex-roommate turned away.

Dewdrop wasn't being pessimistic. Voicing thoughts like that was part of the culture/superstition within the squadron.

"Speaking of the devil, look over there," Welder said.

Coming through the hatch were the Red Force pilots along with some of the squadron officers.

"Why are they coming in here?" Beth asked.

"Check the time. The officer's mess is closed, so if they want to eat before going back to Charlie, they've got to eat here," Dewdrop said.

"Hell, if I were going back to Charlie, I'd wait. They've got a Pepe's there, you know," Hurl said. "Just like at home."

The officers queued up at the serving line. Lieutenant Greenbaum looked up and caught her eye. A smile came over his face as he sauntered over to the table. Beth looked away, refusing to face him.

"Ah, Fire Ant, I'm glad you made your *important* meeting."

She looked up at his smiling face and nodded.

"Well, enjoy your meal, all of you," he said before rejoining the other officers.

"Was that your source?" Dewdrop asked.

Beth nodded.

"Good-looking source, I'd say," her voice loaded with meaning.

"It wasn't like that," she said, and when they laughed, she added, "Oh, just forget it."

She knew she was overreacting. He was standing with the other pilots, and Occam's Razor said that he was a pilot, and he had orders to the Stingers. He'd just been curious about his new unit, given the unusual circumstances in the latest testing.

The squadron was about to move into offensive ops, and she had more to worry about than a curious lieutenant.

Chapter 15

Commodore Ophelia LaRue stood silently as the pilots filed past her to their fighters. Tall with jet black skin, she could almost be the commander's sister—almost. She was a norm with no visible mods, but she had something that their commander didn't have, and that was a cold, calculating presence the chilled the room when she entered. The commander might be a GT with all the typical mannerisms of one born into power, but he obviously cared about the squadron. With the commodore, no one knew where they stood.

Her callsign was Ice, and never was there a more appropriate name. Gollum had served with her in VF-52 when he was a JG, and he'd blanched when the commodore had stepped off the shuttle to take over.

Technically, she'd already been in charge. As the commanding officer of the sector special ops wing, she controlled all the recon scouts, stealth drones, SEAL Teams Two and Eight, and VFX-99. There was probably more in her arsenal as well, classified systems of which Beth knew nothing. As soon as the Stingers were certified, she moved her flag to Sierra Station.

She'd been a foreboding presence, never introducing herself to the squadron. She'd stood silently at the back of the ready room while the mission was briefed, and now she watched as they left for their fighters. Even the commander seemed a little nervous about her presence.

Joshua was all smiles, though, standing alongside the *Tala* as she approached.

"She's purring like a kitten," he said, patting the fuselage. "She'll do you right."

"I know she will," she said as she started her inspection, her plane captain at her elbow.

She trusted Josh completely, but standards were standards, and she went through each step. As expected, she found nothing wrong. She signed for the fighter, and he pulled up the step box he'd had made for her.

A few of her fellow pilots had snickered the first time she'd used it to get into her Wasp, but that rolled right off of her. They were all the same height in the cockpit.

She controlled her excitement. Being too keyed up for extended periods of time could exhaust a pilot, so she ran through her calming techniques. It was difficult, however. This was a real mission, not a training exercise, not being a target drawing enemy fire to be analyzed. They were going out there to kick some ass.

She ran through her pre-flight ops, and everything was green.

"Fox-Four, going hot," she said, miming kissing the cross that lay under her flight suit and against her chest.

"Roger, Fox-Four, going hot."

She gave Josh a thumbs up, and he powered up the initiators. The *Tala* came alive, becoming tumescent, as Mercy used to say in much cruder terms.

She gave a quick look to the next fighter where her ex-roommate was running through her pre-flight ops. They did not speak anymore unless it was work-related, in which case Mercy was the ultimate professional. Beth had finally broken down and told Capgun that there'd been a falling out and asked him if she should transfer to another flight.

Capgun asked if the two could work together, and when Beth had said yes, he told her to let it go. Any sign of discord could get both dropped from the squadron. Beth hadn't been so sure there would be repercussions until the commodore arrived, and after observing her, now she was glad she'd stayed quiet.

Still, she felt a pang in her chest when she thought about what they'd lost.

Just forget it, Floribeth. Do your job.

She pulled up the mission queue again. Beth knew it forward and backward by now, but sitting in the cockpit gave it a whole other perspective. She ran the animation, from launch to the four-gate transit to the strike itself. No plan survived contact with the enemy and the animation had no fewer than six branch plans based on the enemies' reaction.

"T-minus-twenty," the launch chief passed.

Beth had been anxious to get into the *Tala*, but now she wished they'd waited. Twenty minutes didn't seem like much when it was a deadline, but it seemed like forever when sitting waiting to launch. Her bladder let itself be known, but Beth could hold off for now. The smooth piss connection was far more comfortable than the piss tube she'd used in her Hummingbird, but that didn't mean she wanted to have her urine running in the tube that went down her leg and out onto the deck. The Wasp might be high-tech, but without a need to recycle urine for most standard missions, and not wanting it in the fighter where a leak could have consequences, it was simply ejected into the void—or onto the hangar deck.

Ironically, the thought of peeing made her think of not drinking, and that, of course, made her thirsty. She flipped the nipple, then toggled Number Six, taking a swallow of cold Coke.

Josh, my man, I knew I could count on you.

Coke, or any carbonated beverage, was verboten. She understood why. If piss in the cockpit could cause problems, then a pressurized, syrupy liquid could cause even worse ones. He'd hooked her up with Coke before, but with all the engineers crawling over the fighters during the mods, he hadn't been able to load up her dispenser since they arrived, but now, with more freedom and less scrutiny, he'd been able to give her her beverage of choice. She appreciated his efforts, even if she'd never thanked him—never mentioned it, in fact. If she didn't acknowledge it, she didn't have to turn him in—as if that would ever happen.

Gollum locked into her display for a few moments as she checked her readouts, then he was gone. Swordfish had been more hands-on, always asking how everyone was. She respected Swordfish, and she mourned his loss, but it was kind of relaxing that Gollum was not so deep into the weeds. Both were good leaders, but in different ways.

"T-minus ten," the launch chief passed.

Beth checked the tube controls once more. Her FC engine wasn't actually purring, as Joshua had told her. It was more like a tiger, crouching, ready to spring. There was an enormous amount of power there, too much for the hangar to stand up to very many launches, so, as normal, the Wasps would be launched on the cats and not flood their drive tubes until they were a tenth of a megaklick out. Woe behold a pilot if their engine flamed out, though, or their tube flappers jammed. Shot out without power, they would have to wait for a tugdrone to chase them down and haul them back, something no pilot ever wanted to happen. That was a hard thing to live down back in the ready room.

She goosed the engine, then checked the flapper connection. Everything was still green. She should be good to go.

At T-minus-five, Joshua left the hangar deck. Theoretically, he could stand beside the *Tala* as she launched without even mussing his buzz cut, but a launch could be chaotic with all the moving parts, so only the greenshirts were allowed to remain on the deck. All the plane captains and other personnel moved to the far left to the patio.

All except for the commodore, Beth noted. She stood, silent as ever, beside the launch officer. One of the greenshirts came running up with a green vest for her—if she was going to be on the hangar deck during launch, she was supposed to wear it. She waved it off, and the sailor scurried away, the vest still in his hands.

And then it was time. Fox Flight was in the first launch wave. She ran through her lights one more time, mimed kissing her cross again, then with Joshua and the others standing at attention and saluting, the cat kicked in, and she was spat out into space, her compensators straining to counteract the G-forces.

The launch was totally out of her hands. She was on the trajectory assigned to her. At a tenth of a megaklick out, her thumb hovering over the manual flapper control, the automatics kicked in. With a rush of power, the *Tala* came alive.

The mission was on.

Chapter 16

Eight hours after the launch, the mission was scrubbed. The empty sector of space that had been their target had been a dry well. There had been no enemy anywhere within scanner range. They'd all been hyped, pumped up with adrenaline, but they hadn't experienced the release of combat, and that adrenaline sputtered and fizzled as it tried to dissipate.

Well, we'll all make it back, at least, she told herself as she turned over the *Tala* to the AI.

That was a good thing, of course, but she knew it was only delaying the inevitable. A major clash was coming between humans and the NSB-1's, and she'd just as soon start it now before the enemy could react to the new and improved Wasps.

She watched as the *Tala* entered gate lock, then leaned back. Everything was on automatic now. In another two hours and four gate jumps, she'd be back at Sierra, and Josh would be getting the *Tala* ready for the next mission.

She turned the nipple and took another sip of Coke, draining it dry. She'd long ago wet the piss tube, and out here in the black, she didn't care one way or the other, so, she hadn't held back on drinking.

Ahead of her, Alpha was shooting the gate, their blips on her display flaring and then disappearing. As many times as she'd watched it, as many times as she'd made gate jumps, there was still something amazing about the process. One moment, Alpha had been out here in the butt-crack of the Orion Arm, and the next, they were thousands of light years away. At one tiny instant of time, their noses were already there while their asses were still here with Beth and the rest of the squadron.

On her display, she could see the choreography of 40 Wasps, all converging on the single gate. Each four-person flight was approaching from different directions along all three axes. Fox Flight, as the first one through the gate to start the mission, would be the last one to leave. One by one, the other flights shot the gate, passing on to the next leg of the return trip.

The flight before Fox was Romeo, led by the CO. Gates were one-way, and Romeo was approaching from behind and "under" the gate in a sweeping move that pushed the Wasps' maneuverability at this speed. Beth idly watched the four Wasps sweep up in a tight arc, but one of the fighters seemed off. It was the CO himself.

Beth wanted to say something, but it wasn't her place. He was the CO, after all, and each of the remaining pilots still on this side of the gate was senior to her.

"Obsidian, check your approach," Gollum finally passed.

"I've got it," the CO responded in a curt voice

But he didn't. Somehow, incredibly, he missed the gate, and he veered off for a second pass as the other three Romeo fighters shot through.

Beth immediately cut her approach to go chase him, but Gollum passed, "Stay on gate approach. Kilo is coming."

It hurt to do it, but Beth reactivated her gate lock, closing in on it. In 43 seconds and counting, she'd shoot the gate.

To the layman, missing a gate might not seem like much, but at the speeds the Wasps were travelling, and with the potential for enemy contact, it was a big deal. First, it would take a long time before the CO could come around again. Second, Kilo Flight, who was the near-side reaction force, now had to shoot the gate to provide security for him. Third, on the other side of this gate, instead of continuing on to shoot the next gate in their multi-tiered return to Sierra Station, all ten flights that had already gone through had to cool their jets and wait, which messed up the calculations.

The squadron had been ambushed before at TJ-9755 , and Beth had seen how the NSB-1's could seemingly jump into a system from multiple entry points. She stared at her display, afraid to see them appear again here with no one in position to cover the skipper.

Kilo shot the gate ten seconds before Fox did coming in, each Wasp diverting out to clear the way for Fox. Beth didn't want to imagine a head-on collision in space. At the speeds they were traveling, there wouldn't be enough left to vacuum up to send home in an envelope.

But that's why we've got AI's, she thought, then said aloud, "Take care of it, Rose," patting her display.

After quite a bit of teasing, she'd gotten away from anthropomorphizing her AI, but in last-ditch grasp of social defiance, she refused to relinquish her name for hers. Rose was her AI, so screw the rest if they thought naming both her and the *Tala* was weird.

She held her breath, and then she was through. She left control of the *Tala* to Rose. This was where AIs excelled. The intricate dance all the AIs worked in concert was designed to keep at least one flight ready at all times to go back to the CO or shoot the next gate.

Beth kept silent in her cockpit. The CO was out there, alone, with Kilo closing in. Beth, as a scout pilot, had spent days on end alone, but that was before she knew there was an enemy out there. Boredom had been her greatest threat, not death-by-alien.

Time stretched out as she watched her display. She ran a few simulations, and the best the five fighters could manage for a return was just over 36 minutes. At 35, Beth started getting nervous, and that grew as time crept on. Fox Flight's two-minute window within the quadrille to be next up to shoot the gate back if necessary came around, and Beth tensed up, poised to gate lock.

Just before the window passed to Lima Flight, and to her great relief, the CO, followed by Kilo Flight, shot the gate. Within minutes, the AIs were back in control, and they were all back on track, heading to the next leg for their trip back to Sierra Station. Normally, while returning from a mission, there would be banter on the nets, but this time, it was uncomfortably silent.

Beth wasn't sure how the CO had missed the gate. He should have been on gate lock, the approach automatic. She didn't know what could have gone wrong.

She was utterly loyal to the commander. He'd snatched her up from a very bad situation, blamed by the corporation for wiping her AI and facing years of crushing debt. He'd been the one to rescue her, offering her the out by joining the Navy. It was because of him that she flew the *Tala*, the sweetest ship known to humankind.

And he was undoubtedly an extremely capable man, even for a GT. He'd formed the Stingers by sheer force of will, and he'd prepared the squadron to protect humanity. Most GTs had a political bent, and the CO was no exception, all to the good of the squadron. He'd been able to get what was needed and navigate the intricate dance that modern politics demanded.

What he wasn't was a good pilot. Too tall by almost 20 centimeters, he barely fit into his Wasp—no, not barely—he *didn't* fit. His upraised knees blocked part of the view of his display. He must hurt like a son-of-a-bitch on the long missions, all cramped up like that. Even on short training missions, he wasn't a good pilot, and his comp scores were always the lowest in the squadron.

It wasn't like he was a liability—at least, Beth hadn't thought so before this. There was no getting around it now, however. After missing the gate, he'd put himself and Kilo at risk. If he had been a norm, if he'd been an enlisted pilot, he'd probably just earned getting his wings pulled. But he was neither: he was a well-connected commanding officer, and more pertinent, he was of the Golden Tribe.

Like almost every norm, Beth had mixed feelings about GTs. They were beautiful, had a commanding presence, and they were always projected in a positive light in the media. But they were different, and they wielded immense power given their small numbers. That created no small degree of resentment. Everyone dreamed of being a GT, but they also harbored misgivings about them.

Commander Tuominen was a good person, though, and Beth's mixed feelings about him had nothing to do with him being a GT. On the one hand, she wanted him to remain as CO, but on the other hand, she also was concerned about what just happened. Fighter pilots had to rely on each other, they had to know that their wingmen had their six. The Commander's heart was in the right place, but he just might not have the capability to be an effective pilot.

Her mind drifted on the way back, only half-monitoring the three jumps. She was almost surprised when STC took over her final approach into Sierra Station. Beth felt the tractors take over and she shut down the engines. She was exhausted, more so than she'd have felt had she been in combat. More than that, she was disappointed.

As the *Tala* entered the hangar, Beth could see the commodore, standing like a specter watching her minions return from her bidding. Beth couldn't contain the shudder that ran through her.

The *Tala* was tractored in to her apron where Joshua stood waiting, already studying the readout. As her canopy retracted, he asked if she had anything to add.

"No issues," she said.

"OK, then. I should have her checked and up in thirty."

She climbed out of her Wasp, leaving her to Joshua's tender ministrations. Capgun met her as she stepped off.

"What do you make of that?" he asked her.

She didn't have to ask to what "that" referred.

"I don't know. You've been flying for a lot longer than I have. What do you think?"

"I've been flying longer, but I've never seen anything like that," he said as Mercy joined them.

"Here he comes," Mercy said, pointing.

All three looked on as the CO's Wasp floated into the hangar. All around them, other pilots stopped and watched as well as his fighter settled on the deck, the commodore standing in front of the apron. The canopy retracted, and like some giant, long-legged insect, the CO unfolded himself and stepped out. He stepped up to the commodore, listened intently to her for a moment, and then the two turned and walked off of the flight deck.

The three pilots watched in silence until the two passed through the hatch and out of the hangar. Capgun let out a heavy sigh, then walked off. For a moment, Beth and Mercy stood alone together. Beth wondered if she should say anything, but she was saved from making that decision by Mercy leaving.

She wasn't sure if she was relieved or disappointed.

Turning back to the *Tala*, Joshua was sitting in the cockpit, going over his checklist. No matter what was going on with the CO, life in the Navy kept on chugging along. In another hour, in another day, in another week—Beth would be going back out to face the enemy. The only thing she could control was how well she was prepared to do her duty.

With a sigh almost as loud as Capgun's had been, she left Joshua to his work.

Chapter 17

"I'd just feel better if you had a desk job," Beth's mother said. "I don't like you out there in space who-knows-where all alone."

"Nanay, I was all alone in my Hummingbird when I was with Hamandani Brothers."

"I know, and I didn't like that, either. But now, you're in the Navy. Wanda's boy, George, he's in the Navy now, too, and he's going to be a storekeeper. That's a good job, and when he gets out, he can start a business here."

Beth's eyes wanted to roll, but she controlled herself. Her ina was just being a mother.

"You forget, Nanay, that I get flight pay as a pilot. George won't be getting anything like that."

"All the money in the galaxy won't do us any good if your little ship doesn't bring you back, love. You talk to your commander, OK? See if you can switch jobs."

Oh, yeah, I'm sure I'm going to do that.

Spartan mothers probably said the same thing to their sons thousands of years ago. It was just something to endure.

"Maybe when this tour is over," she said, unwilling to argue. "Well, I need to get back, so I'll try to call next week. I love you all."

The gathered family all waved and gave her their love. Just before she cut off, a little pink light lit up at the bottom of the comms display. Rocky, who was tied into the call at his little apartment over the store, wanted to talk privately.

She blew kisses to the family and waited for them to cut the connection. She had an idea as to what Rocky wanted, and while prepared for it, she was not looking forward to this.

"OK, Rocky. We're alone. What is it?"

He looked pensive, which just cemented what she'd surmised.

"Ate, is everything OK over there?" he asked. "Mercy—"

"Yes, Mercy. I wanted to talk to you about her. Everything's fine, but you know, Mercy, well, she's been busy, and, well, she . . . she might have other things on her mind, so you shouldn't be expecting her to call you."

"What?" he asked, is eyebrows scrunched in confusion. "She calls me almost every day."

"She does?" she asked, totally taken aback. "Every day?"

"Well, not every day. I know you've got your training missions. But almost every day. What did you mean about her calling me? What other things does she have on her mind. Is she OK?" he asked in a rush.

"Yes, she's fine," Beth said.

She'd been taken off guard. She'd been so sure that Mercy would have dropped Rocky by now and had practiced how she would console him, that finding out that they were still communicating had thrown her off her game plan.

"Well, OK, but then the question is are *you* OK?"

Now she was even more confused.

"Yes, I'm OK. Why are you asking?"

"Well, every time I ask Mercy about you, she doesn't seem completely forthcoming. She says you're fine, but it's like she's avoiding the question. If I ask her for any details, she talks around the subject."

So, she hasn't told him we've had a falling out.

"So, what's up? Are you OK? Is there something wrong? You can tell me, Ate. I won't go running to Nanay."

"Uh . . . no, Rocky. Everything's fine. Really. I mean, the training tempo is high . . ."

She had to watch what she said. The scanbots were monitoring every conversation leaving the station, and they'd cut the connection should the AIs determine that the talk was getting too close to the classified truth.

" . . . but we're all doing well. Mercy too," she added, feeling guilty for throwing that in.

She didn't know if Mercy was fine. She was performing fine, and they still flew well together, but as far as her personal life? She didn't know.

"Are you sure? I'm serious. You can always tell me."

He was probably right, she knew. Maybe not for this as it looked like he was still involved, and it wouldn't be right to lay her problems with Mercy at his feet. But Rocky was a sweet soul with a surplus of compassion and empathy.

That was why she was so pissed at Mercy. If Mercy had taken a shining to Gary, her kuya, which meant older brother, she wouldn't have cared, and probably would have told them to have a great time. Rocky was different, though, and she couldn't bear to see him hurt.

"I know I can tell you, and if there was anything to tell, I would. But there isn't. Everything's fine."

Across the light years, Rocky stared into the pickup as if trying to lay her soul bare. For a moment, she wished this was seventy years ago before real-time comms were possible.

Finally, he shrugged, then said, "OK, Ate, if you say so. Just take care, OK? And say hello to Mercy."

Beth kissed the tips of her fingers and put them up on the pickup lens.

"You take care, little brother."

She cut the link, not exactly sure what this all meant.

Chapter 18

Beth strode through the passage, head down, oblivious to anyone else. She was pissed. Everyone in the squadron was pissed, and morale was suffering. She'd just been on another 12-hour goat-rope with nothing to show for it. Since becoming certified two weeks ago, she'd been out on six missions, all dry wells. It was as if the NSB-1s had disappeared from the galaxy. Not one of them believed that to be the case, though.

It was rough. To continually get up for a mission, then have nothing happen, was wearing them down. Hurl and Comet had gotten into a fight, of all things, in the mess decks. Both were now spending their time on head duty for the next week when they weren't flying, and this time, Beth approved of the command master chief's decision.

Hurl was lucky it had been Comet. The argument had been between three of them, and Tikihead was an officer. If Hurl had punched him, it would have resulted in the brig instead of merely scrubbing shitters.

She passed another pilot, not bothering to look up. All she wanted to do now was to take a hot sonicshower and get out of her funk.

"Hey, Fire Ant!" the other pilot said.

She looked up and took a deep breath to compose herself. It was Lieutenant Greenbaum, and she was not in the mood for his prying.

"Sir?" she said before she noticed the red flight suit, the bright red of the Stingers rather than the deep red of the Red

Force pilots. "Oh, are you here now?" she said, asking the obvious.

He pointed at the Stinger patch on his shoulder and laughed, saying, "I'm one of you now, and I have to say, it's been eye-opening. I know why you were being reticent when I caught you after the mission debrief."

"Sir?" she said again.

She hadn't heard that the new joins had arrived, and it was still possible that he was DOI and was testing security.

"I mean why you couldn't tell me. Aliens, of all things. I mean, we knew something was up, but aliens? Really?"

"So, you know now?" she asked, once again stating the obvious.

"Yeah, all briefed up. We went over your missions, too. You're quite the pilot, Fire Ant. Very impressive."

Beth felt her face turn red, and she stammered out, "Not really. I just was doing my job. We lost some good people."

"Yeah, Swordfish. He was good people—a good pilot, too. I thought it was fishy that he supposedly was killed in a training accident. Now, I understand," he said soberly.

"You knew him?"

Oh, come on, Floribeth! Quit questioning the obvious. He just said Swordfish was "good people."

"We were Academy classmates together. I didn't know him that well when we were there, but we became closer at flight school. But don't sell yourself short. What you did with that Hummingbird, that was epic."

"They told you about that, too?" she asked, surprised.

"We went over every human-NSB-1 encounter. Yours was the first one. Fine, fine piloting."

Beth was feeling very self-conscious. She tried to sense any sarcasm in the lieutenant's voice. Some of the officers still thought enlisted pilots were a mistake, and that without university degrees, they could never match up to them. Most pilots, not just the officers, were dismissive of Hummingbirds and other civilian craft. But if he was playing her, he was hiding it well.

"I'm going to want to hear your take on that mission. Well, the one in SC9222, too. When you get the time, give me a chance to pick your brain."

"Uh . . . sure, sir."

"Come on, we're squadron mates now. I'm Cossack. Unless you insist I call you Naval Enlisted Pilot Third Class Floribeth . . . uh, what is your last name? I forgot it."

"Dalisay. Floribeth Salinas O'Shea Dalisay, sir."

"So, is that what you want me to call you?"

"Uh, no sir. Fire Ant is just fine."

"Then Cossack is fine, too."

Even in the squadron, this was more than she'd spoken to any officer on a social basis, and she was feeling uncomfortable, but it was a tradition to use callsigns for addressing each other, so it really wasn't out of the ordinary. Still, she wanted to change the subject.

"So, when do you get your ride?"

"Tomorrow," he said, a smile taking over his face. "I'm in the first group of twelve. We start snapping in on Wednesday while the next twelve get theirs."

"Twenty-four? We've got twenty-four new pilots?"

"No, Fire Ant, not twenty-four."

"But you said the 'next twelve.'"

"Yes, I did. But we've got fifty new pilots who've reported aboard, plus ground crew."

That staggered her. Another 50 pilots?

"You didn't know?" he asked, seeing her expression.

"No. I mean, I knew we were getting some new pilots, but not fifty."

"And it isn't going to end there. Another fifty are slated after us."

"But, Sierra Station only has 70 aprons," she said. "Where's everyone going to be put?"

"I know this just got approved, and you've been out on a mission, but they really need to promulgate the word better. Not all of the upgraded Wasps will be here. We'll have squadrons with First, Third, and Fifth Fleets for now. Within 120 days, there'll be 300 Wasps modified for combat with the NSB-1's. That doesn't include the capital ships."

"Capital ships?"

"Yeah. A couple of destroyers and cruisers and the *Victory*, to start off with.

"The *Victory*? That's a battle carrier."

The *Victory* was one of only five new battle carriers, each one capable of carrying an entire fighter wing as well as a reinforced regiment of Marines. They'd never been used in a full-scale war, and their mere presence was usually enough to put out any brush fires.

If a battle carrier was getting the mods, that could only mean one thing.

"We're taking the fight to the FALs," she said quietly as it sunk in.

"Total war."

Chapter 19

"Here you go," Bull said, pulling a burger off the grill and onto her plate. "You want a pongee, too?"

"No, the burger'll do fine," Beth said.

"You need to eat more. Get some meat on your bones," he said.

"Hell, Bull, you should be glad she's about as big as an ant, or your fat ass would still be back at 9222, heading out into the deep black," Ranger said, poking him in the ribs with his spoon. He turned to Beth and said, "But now that he mentioned it, how about some of these brownies? Made them myself, you know."

"Bullshit," Bull protested. "I'm within weight standards, and if you made those brownies, then I'll kiss your smelly feet."

"Get on down there and start kissing, Bull."

"Yeah, give me two of them, Ranger," Beth said, shaking her head in amusement.

The two were best friends, but they were constantly going after each other like a 50-year married couple.

Beth stole a glance at Mercy, four people ahead of her in the serving line. They'd lasted only five months as friends.

"Hey, how come she got two?" one of the new joins asked, someone whose name Beth didn't even know yet. "You said I have to come back for seconds after everyone's done."

"She's earned two," Bull said before he went back to Ranger, telling him that dialing in "brownies" on the food fabricator did not constitute "making" them.

Beth stuck out her tongue at the new join, surprising herself, then burst out laughing.

Yeah, I earned them. What have you done?

He could have won the Fletcher Award, for all she knew, but that was the problem. She didn't know him, and she didn't know many of the new joins.

This was Commander Tuominen's answer to that problem. He was still the commanding officer, thank goodness, although rumors were rampant as to his flight status. With the new joins, he had decided that a steel beach BBQ would be a good ice-breaker between the new and old within the over-sized squadron. The hangar had been set up with grills and tables, and the mess chief had provided a pretty good spread, with the original Stingers doing the serving to the new. Fox Flight had helped set up the tables, so the four of them were now free to eat as well.

The current plan was to keep the enlarged squadron together while the new pilots snapped in. Then, the squadron would be split, with some of the old flights moving to a new squadron, to be replaced by some of the new pilots. Commander Tuominen would retain VFX-99, and Commander Nanet "Griffen" Urkirk would take command of the new VFX-51.

The purpose of the BBQ was to intermingle, but with the crowded deck, where some of the Wasps did not even have their own aprons, it was easy to get compartmentalized. Beth found herself with Hurl and some of the plane captains and techs who she knew and with whom she felt comfortable. She'd formed a casual relationship with Glorya Leung, based on too many hours spent together on head-cleaning duty. Beth knew that Glorya had a bit of a case of hero-worship for her, and that was more than a little ego-inflating. Beyond that, she just liked her. Glorya had been busted down to Seaman Recruit for socking her petty officer, and while Beth didn't condone that kind of thing, still, it made the quiet young woman something of an enigma to her.

The BBQ might not be doing what is was supposed to in mixing the two groups, but as Beth looked around, she knew it was still a good thing. The stress level within the squadron was climbing. Every single one of the pilots just wanted to break their combat cherry as a modified squadron, and each dry well was mentally taxing.

Listen to those two geeks, she thought affectionately, looking at Hurl and Josh as they argued about some arcane rules of magic in one of the games into which they regularly immersed themselves.

Gigi, Hurl's plane captain, interjected herself into the argument, giving yet a third opinion. Beth had tried to play "Poseidon 3" with their gaming group once, but she'd been quickly lost in all the rules and had floundered, getting killed after only 20 minutes.

She took a bite of her second brownie. She probably agreed with Bull in that pushing a button on a fabricator did not constitute "making" them, but even still, these were pretty darned good.

She craned her neck to see the chow line, wondering if there were any more left.

Only one way to find out, she told herself as she stood up.

She hadn't even taken a step when the hangar lights started flashing red, and an excited voice on the 1MC blared out, "Pilots, Alert Status 1A. Flight leaders, to the ready room, now!"

Everyone stood stark still for a second before they started running for the lockers. Some of the newly-joined pilots hesitated, then a voice rang out, "Training Flights, this does not mean you. Keep out of the way!"

Beth bolted for the lockers, dropping her plate in the trash can as she ran by. Alert Status 1A meant in their Wasps, ready to launch. Something was up, something big.

The locker was all elbows and knees. Beth whipped off her overalls, then got knocked on her ass by someone as she struggled with her flight suit. She didn't bother getting up. It was easier just to pull it on down low, then crawl out from under the legs of her fellow pilots. She was the second pilot to reach the aprons. Josh was already there, running the startups.

Normally, she'd have to inspect the *Tala*, but for Alert Status 1A, that requirement was waived. Josh would do whatever he could in the time she might have.

Looking forward, the new-joins and squadron staff were hauling away tables and chairs, clearing the launch. Cossack was one of them, and when he looked back and caught her eye, he gave her a thumbs up before turning back to the task at hand.

Four minutes after the alarm sounded, half of the pilots were in their Wasps while the launch crew prepared the catapults. Three minutes after that, the flight leaders came running out of the ready room. Gollum's *Lucky Lucy* was just to Beth's left, and she watched as he climbed up into the cockpit.

He slammed on his helmet, and a moment later, passed, "Innamincka Station and Toowoomba are currently under attack by the NSB-1's. We're scrambling right now to relieve the station."

Beth felt a surge of adrenaline flow through her, sparking her nerves alight. There wasn't going to be a dry well this time. This was the real deal.

UNCHARTED SPACE

Chapter 20

Beth studied the readout as she waited for the go-ahead for the final gate. Without time for a formal operations brief, bits and pieces were being uploaded to the Wasps as they were developed.

Innamincka Station was an industrial processing plant in the Toowoomba system. Toowoomba was nearly Earth-normal, with extensive mineral resources and a minimal axial tilt that provided for steady and calm weather. The weather didn't make much difference to the mining, but it made the planet a superb platform for agriculture and ranching.

Over a million people lived in the station, while fewer than 200,000 were on the planet's surface. The mines and ranches were highly automated, which was why the population was relatively low.

Even combining the two populations, the Toowoomba system was barely a blip in the breadth of humanity. There were more people living within 50 klicks of Beth's hometown of San Miguel.

Toowoomba had just cemented itself firmly into human history, however, and not in a way anyone would have wanted. Just over two hours ago, the NSB-1's had attacked the station with over 40 ships. Communications with both the station and the planet were intermittent, and the reporting was spotty, but from what was reported, large portions of the station were destroyed. Beth didn't want to think of the loss of life that must have occurred.

And the squadron still didn't have a firm ops order. They were going to shoot the next gate into the system with only the basic idea of what they were going to do.

This was never a good idea. The Navy worked best through close coordination, and this was considered their primary force multiplier. This, along with better technology, was the main reason why smaller numbers of Navy ships almost always defeated even larger groups. Pirates, for example, just didn't have the capability to act as one integrated unit to the same degree.

Time, however, precluded much in the way of preparation. The Stingers were going to have to rely on their training to get the job done.

Beth shifted her attention to the order of battle. Nothing there had changed. Fox Flight was to be the fourth flight through the gate. Their tentative approach to Innamincka Station was from below the elliptic and the station's port side. All of that depended on the enemy situation, though. As soon as they shot the gate, they had to be flexible to meet the threat.

Beth's heart was pounding in her chest, and she just wanted to get into it. The waiting was too hard on her. With humans dying in the system, she wanted to take the gate in the minimum two jumps, but security procedures were still in effect. No one knew exactly how the NSB-1's navigated through space, and no one knew what capabilities they had to track human jumps, so all jumps into contact had to go through an unmanned way station gate complex that had been set up deep inside the Orion Arm, far from any human planets. A gate drone had already set up a gate linking to the Toowoomba gate. If the NSB-1's were somehow able to track from where the squadron jumped, it would be from a non-populated chunk of space, not from Sierra Station.

That meant that if the enemy could follow them through the Toowoomba gate, they'd be stuck at the way station. The gates back to human space would be powered down, to be opened only after the gate from Toowoomba was closed. That also meant that they couldn't make the jump into the Toowoomba system until all craft were there at the staging area.

The Stingers were all there, waiting to attack, but a monitor and a destroyer were still enroute. The Stingers could not commence their rescue efforts until the other two arrived and the gates into the way station were powered down.

Beth wasn't sure how effective the other two vessels would be. There had been the system monitor in place, of course, but from what was gleaned from the messages, the big orbital platform had been destroyed, which was a bitter pill to swallow. Monitors were massive hunks of pure power, with four immense guns capable of taking on almost any ship known to man.

Remotely operated by sailors in a secret base on a secret station somewhere, the unmanned monitors were extremely difficult to knock out—yet that had been the fate of the system monitor. Beth just hoped it managed to take out a bunch of NSB-1's with it. But if that monitor had been taken down, then why did the brass think that a new one would survive any better?

Still, she had to admit that a monitor's four cannons packed more of a punch than any ten Wasps.

As did the destroyer, but none of the capital ships had been modified yet. Depending on the class , one destroyer could carry upwards of 400 torpedoes—Beth quickly pulled up the *DS Wysocki*. She was a Guling-Class destroyer, and she carried 370 of them. She had three different types of cannons, making her far more powerful than a Wasp in ship-to-ship combat, but she was also not nearly as maneuverable, and in this case, she did not have the new mods.

While the commander, XO, and flight leaders took advantage of the delay to try and tweak the plan, as little as it was, the rest of the pilots simply waited while humans were probably being killed, just a gate away.

The *Wysocki* arrived first, and Beth had to admit that she felt better with the ship there. The destroyer was not going to enter the Toowoomba system unless absolutely necessary. Her mission was to make sure none of the NSB-1's made it past the way station if things went south.

It took another fifteen minutes, fifteen in which thousands of humans could have died, before the monitor joined them. The plan was still tentative and basic, but they couldn't wait any longer.

It was time to go on the offensive.

TOOWOOMBA SYSTEM

Chapter 21

Beth mimed kissing her cross, then held her breath as the *Tala* shot the gate. An instant later, she was in the Toowoomba system, her preprogrammed route whipping her "down" in the elliptical plane and to her left. The Toowoomba gate was quite near Innamincka Station, less than two megaklicks away, and the station shone like a diamond reflecting the system's sun. Beyond the station, the planet itself loomed large.

Like all Navy ships, Wasps could fight at incredibly long distances, but they excelled at the shorter-ranged fights, so this was right in their wheelhouse. She ran her thumb over the manual trigger release for the railgun, glad she had it again. The fireturd system had been switched over to an external pod.

Her combat display lit up with bogeys around the station. The local space guard, which was intended to hold off raiders and pirates, had IFF, and Beth prayed that some of the bogeys would sort out as them. After ten seconds, it was obvious that whatever space guard force had been there before was gone. Each of the bogeys shifted to the red of bandits. There were 42 of them, swarming around the station in no discernable pattern.

And there are 40 of us.

"Fox Flight, diamond on me," Gollum passed, his voice calm and collected. "These are our designated targets, but do not acquire target lock. Weapons are free. I repeat weapons are free."

Beth jinked the *Tala* over into position off the flight leader's port side as they started sweeping up. She held her fire, as did all of the pilots. The monitor, following the quicker Wasps, however, immediately started to open up, the traces of its cannons showing up in yellow on her display.

The NSB-1's immediately reacted. Fifteen, seemingly drawn at random and not from a single unit, peeled out of the swarm and headed to the monitor.

"Fox, come . . . wait one," Gollum said, followed by, "Belay that. Continue on present course."

Kilo and Echo Flights broke their approach with a course to flank the 15 enemy. Eight against fifteen didn't seem like good odds, but the station was the priority at the moment. Besides, the monitor went a long way in evening up those odds.

Beth couldn't watch them. She had to focus on what was ahead of them, and it was the NSB-1's who bit first. A wave of particle beams swept the *Tala*, sending the internal sirens howling.

"Keep on me," Gollum shouted. "Commence firing beamers."

"As before, Beth and Capgun's beamers were on single pulses while Gollum and Mercy were in nano-mode. Jean-Luc and his team were convinced that mixing it up confused the enemy. Beth wasn't sure how they'd come up with that theory, but she gave them the benefit of the doubt. They'd been pretty much spot on so far.

Beth got hit twice more as they closed in still on a straight-on approach. Her shields were holding steady, down only 12%. The *Tala* was holding up well, but she wasn't here to merely survive. She was here to kill FALs, and her beamers didn't seem to be having much effect.

That wasn't entirely true. Their targets started what looked to be erratic maneuvering, and that could be in response to their beamers.

As the two sides closed, the aliens fired their torpedoes—which closed awfully fast. Jean-Luc thought the new shields would provide some protection from the torps, but he wasn't sure, and that didn't give Beth a warm and fuzzy. She had to shift her beamer from targeting the crystals to the torpedoes.

She kept watching the range close as the enemy torps sped to meet them. She waited for Gollum to order them to break, but the order never came. Finally, the first torp was taken out, followed in quick succession by six more. The last one evidently had target lock on the *Tala*, but with combined fire, it was taken out at nine kiloklicks—way, way too close for comfort.

In response, Fox Flight launched their torpedoes, a salvo of four. Beth's was destroyed, but Gollum's made it through to splash one of the bandits.

The other three whooped over the net, and Gollum had to tell them to focus. There was still lots of fighting ahead of them.

As the two opposing forces maneuvered, Fox Flight passed within four kiloklicks of the station.

"Hell, look at that," Capgun said.

Beth pulled up the visuals, then sucked in a breath. The station was a junkyard. The wreckage was evident, and gasses were venting from a hundred points. How anyone could survive that . . .

"Focus," Gollum said, cutting the visuals on their displays. "We can't worry about that now. We're coming around for another pass."

The dogfight was a ballet of sorts, but a slowly moving ballet that took time to develop. They were flying much slower this close to the planet, so they were able to maneuver more rapidly within the battle area, but still, the distances involved were much greater than typically depicted in the holovids. While the targeting AI's dueled to adjust shield frequencies at up to a couple of thousand times per second, the actual fighting took place over longer periods of time.

As they emerged from the corkscrew Gollum had led them through, they were in a better position to engage again. Three of the aliens had been their target, but another three passed into their target cone as well, so now they had six. Each of them fired another torpedo, then followed that with beamer fire. The maneuvering became more violent as the aliens tried to break lock while the humans tried to keep it.

Except that the aliens were not just on the defensive. Alarms blasted as their heat weapon engaged the *Tala*. The temperature started to rise, and rise quickly. Beth could try and break lock, but that would also break hers on her target ship.

The enemy heat weapon also degraded their own beamers. Her fireturds started shooting out, and her temperatures steadied. Now it was just a matter of how many fireturds she had left.

Her target jinked, breaking lock. Without a target lock anymore, Beth jinked, too, breaking the lock on her as well. The enemy would be tracking her, but she should be able to be a step ahead of it. Even at these close ranges, it still took the beams time to reach them, time in which they could maneuver out of the way.

But sometimes, luck was against a pilot, and jinking right instead of left put a Wasp right into a concentrated beam as it arrived. When that happened enough times, bad things happened.

"Shit, I'm hit bad," Mercy passed.

"What's your status?" Gollum asked. "I'm not getting readouts."

"Shields gone, leaking gammas. Fuck. All systems bent. I'm winchester."

"Can you return through the gate to the *Wysoki*?"

There was a pause, then, "Negative. Life support's failing."

"The station! How about the station?" Beth interjected as another heat beam enveloped her.

The *Tala* was already hot, and immediately, her fireturds started shooting out. Beth pulled into a tight turn to try and shake the bandit and position herself for another torpedo shot.

"Nothing left there," Capgun said. "We saw it."

"Ditch to the planet. We'll pick you up after," Gollum ordered Mercy.

Beth was intent on breaking free of the heat beam, but her heart was in her throat with Mercy on her mind. The four Wasps were travelling too fast to enter Toowoomba's atmosphere. Mercy would need to take half-a-dozen orbits to reach a safe speed, and she didn't have time for that. She'd be out of O2 long before she could complete the orbits. It would be bad enough if her Wasp were whole, but with it damaged, no one knew if it could take the buffeting without coming apart. But she didn't know what Mercy's options were.

She passed out of the enemy beam's reach and fired her second torpedo at the bandit. Immediately, the bandit broke hard down, sweeping back at the torpedo.

Smart move, she had to admit. Given the close distance, there was no way the torpedo could cut it off in time.

"Roger. I'm heading down," Mercy said.

"Fire Ant, cover her."

"Roger that."

Only another bandit was on her, and he had her locked in. Her temp started spiking, and her fireturds commenced ejecting like automatic tracer fire. She pulled in hard, but the bandit had her inside, and she couldn't break free. The *Tala* was getting closer and closer to failure.

"Splash one," Capgun said, then on the 1P, "And you're welcome, Fire Ant. You owe me one, and we're tied now."

Her temps started to fall as the fireturds transferred energy out into the void.

Beth had been more than a little proud that with her two kills, she had the most in the squadron. Now, Capgun was tied with her, and she thanked her lucky stars for that. In ten or twenty more seconds, she might have been the one splashed.

"Yeah, I owe you, Capgun. Hit me up on the rebound," she said as she brought the *Tala* around to follow Mercy.

There was a flash on her display.

Shit!

The monitor had been taken out. With ten . . . no, now eleven, she saw . . . with eleven Wasps down, the monitor had been a huge portion of their firepower. Facing them were 28 bandits.

Most pilots thought poorly of drone pilots, sitting safe and sound back on their secret base, but whoever had been on that monitor had been shit-hot. Beth hoped she'd survive long enough to buy that pilot a beer sometime.

Without a bandit immediately on her ass, she locked onto Mercy, then started after her. Gollum and Capgun wheeled about and headed back to the ruined station.

"I've got your six," she passed on the 1P. There was no answer. "Mercy, do you read me?" Still nothing.

"Her comms are out," she muttered.

It didn't really matter. Mercy wasn't going to have a hard-enough time as it was, and whether she knew Beth was there or not wouldn't change what she had to do. She goosed the *Tala* ahead to close within a half a kiloklick as Mercy started down a steep entry.

Mercy was going in too hot, though. She could easily break apart at these speeds, and she wasn't slowing down. Beth ran some quick calculations. If Mercy survived, then her current trajectory should land her in the vicinity of one of the planet's refineries.

That was a very rough estimate. With her Wasp damaged, it would be impossible to pinpoint a location where she'd land, and "in the vicinity" could mean anywhere within 100 klicks. She didn't even know if that was one of the automated plants or a manned one, but it was probably better than nothing.

Beth checked her display. Golf Flight was battling five bandits, and Gollum and Capgun were heading their way.

"Come on, Hurl, keep fighting," she muttered as she did her cross kissing simulation.

She turned back to Mercy. She'd be back in the fight soon enough, but at the moment, she had to make sure her flightmate made it down, then mark her position.

Ahead of her, a small glow appeared. Beth was puzzled for a moment before she realized that it was Mercy, just entering the exosphere. She was surprised she could see it with her naked eyes. Half a kiloklick was nothing in space terms, but in an atmosphere, that was a long distance.

"Keep it together, Mercy," she muttered.

She goosed the *Tala* again, jumping up two-tenths of a kiloklick. Now, just 300 klicks ahead, she could see a bright glow as Mercy's Wasp continued to heat. For the first time, the *Tala* shuddered as well as she kissed the exosphere, too.

As long as the glow ahead stayed relatively compact, she knew Mercy's Wasp was still intact. She could only hope that inside of it, Mercy was still alive.

Beth was travelling too fast to follow Mercy down, but that just highlighted the danger Mercy was in. A couple of hundred klicks above her, Beth adjusted her track for an orbit of the planet.

"Gollum, Red Devils' still intact, but descending fast. I've got too much speed, so, I'm taking an orbit before coming back around and trying to spot her landing."

"Roger that. Record, then rejoin us."

Beth whipped past Mercy below her, bleeding speed to give her time to reach the ground. She kept her scanners on Mercy until the bulk of the planet blocked her.

Toowoomba was a very pretty planet from space, but Beth didn't notice. She just hoped that Mercy would still be intact as the *Tala* came back around. With her heart in her throat, she watched the scanner, praying. She almost cried out with relief when she saw the blip on her scanners, and she tagged her visuals to see the far-off Wasp, trailing smoke, but still intact.

Another blip caught her attention, and for a moment, she thought that somehow, a SAR bird was already there to pick her up when she landed. But that was impossible. There were no SAR birds on this . . .

Shit! It's a bandit.

Somehow, a bandit had appeared, two hundred klicks from Mercy and closing in.

How . . .

How didn't matter. There was no doubt in Beth's mind that the bandit was going to shoot Mercy out of the sky.

Beth was travelling slower, at the edge of the exosphere, but she was still flying too fast to safely enter it. A glow was flowing past her canopy, and the *Tala* was bouncing. Mercy was in the thermosphere still far above the planet's surface. Beth had to get the bandit off Mercy's ass, but if she took another orbit to bleed off more speed, the bandit would splash her long before Mercy could land.

This was an easy choice to make. The remaining fighters *might* need her in the continuing fight, but Mercy *did* need her.

"I'm going in," she passed to Gollum. "Red Devil's got a bandit on her."

She cut her comms, which was probably a court-martial offense, but she was afraid that Gollum would order her to break contact, and she'd rather deal with breaking comms than disobeying a direct order.

Turning the *Tala* in, she dove deeper into the exosphere, her alarms chiming to tell her this was not a good idea. The buffeting was teeth jarring, and she was glad for the harness that kept her firmly in place. She didn't know just how much cushion was built into the specs, but if Mercy was still flying with her damaged Wasp, then the *Tala* should be able to handle it.

She hoped.

A golden glow surrounded her as she burned through the atmosphere, and that interfered with her sensors. Her display took the bits of data that made it through to monitor Mercy and the bandit, so this wasn't a vital issue, but Beth felt blind, like riding a bike facing into the setting sun—riding the bike over an *extremely* bumpy road. It could be done, but it was disconcerting.

She wanted to speed up, but excess speed was the enemy in atmospheric combat. Too fast, and she not only lost maneuverability, but she could put the *Tala* through too much stress. At high speed, the atmosphere could be like concrete. Come in too fast, and she'd be limited to one pass. Come in too slow, and she'd be too late.

Her mind raced as she plunged down, closing the gap. Her torpedoes were useless within an atmosphere and gravity well. Her beamer could be used, but a Wasp was not a capital ship or a monitor with multi-gigajoule cannons. Her relatively small cannon would take longer to defeat an opponent. Dogfights with beamers usually turned into a fight of attrition—whoever could accumulate more time with the weapon on the other won. She had the enemy fighter in range now, but she was afraid that if she fired, the bandit would immediately splash Mercy.

Beth was surprised that the bandit hadn't taken Mercy under fire yet. She had to be within its range.

That left her railgun. She knew it was an effective weapon against the alien craft—one of her kills had been using it. She just needed to be able to run the firing solutions. Without all the atmospheric data and planet specs, her targeting AI would be giving a best-guess estimate, and coupled with the buffeting of the *Tala*, that could result in a miss that would be just as bad as alerting the bandit with her beamer.

Her targeting AI kept running firing solutions for the railgun, narrowing it down as the range closed and more data came in. It now gave Beth a 39% probability of success, and that was climbing with each minute.

She'd slowed down significantly, and the buffeting eased up a bit. The corona that surrounded her began to have momentary gaps that allowed her to see out. Switching her visuals to the bandit, getting her first real glimpse of the enemy. The models she'd seen back at Sierra Station were pretty spot on. It looked like crystals gone wild, like a high school project that had gone haywire. Angles and shards stuck up at seemingly random angles. It didn't make sense, and all those protuberances should make atmospheric flying more difficult, but it sure seemed to be flying without a problem.

Beth still didn't know why it hadn't fired upon Mercy yet. Surely the Wasp was in its range. Unless . . .

Hell. It doesn't want to destroy her, it wants to capture her! she thought with sudden conviction.

It made sense. Both craft had slowed down quite a bit, and they were getting closer to the surface. The alien could wait and splash Mercy closer to the ground, then go in and pick up the pieces. Mercy was not maneuvering her Wasp at all, so she probably didn't know she had a bandit on her ass and would be making it easy for it to take her out even after landing.

Beth didn't want to think of the other possibility. Mercy might not be maneuvering because she was dead, not having survived entry.

Whatever explanation was correct, Beth knew she had to keep Mercy's Wasp out of the enemy's hands. She had to be willing to destroy the Navy fighter if it came to that.

The *Tala* entered the thermosphere, still flying wickedly fast, but within parameters. That was one less worry for Beth, but the main worries still loomed largely, and she was running out of time to make a decision.

An image flashed in her mind, of her first dogfight with Fox Flight against the Red Force. She'd delayed firing her beamers until the optimal moment, and that had cost her. She'd been knocked out of the exercise before she could fire. She'd sworn then she'd never be caught like that again.

Her probability of a kill had now risen to 64%, but her mind was already made up. She triggered the railgun, sending a stream of hypervelocity depleted uranium slugs at the bandit. The first burst missed, passing just in front of the bandit. That extra data was all the AI needed. It adjusted, using the "Kentucky Windage," and fired another stream which would have hit the bandit dead-on—if the bandit had cooperated by remaining on course.

Almost the instant the first rounds passed in front of the bandit, it performed and almost impossible maneuver, dodging up and to Beth's right.

"Bastard! I'm on you, though!"

A heat beam hit her as she took the *Tala* into a Split-S so she could boom-and-zoom on the lower-altitude enemy, and the warning sirens blared, but the *Tala* was heating up less despite the heat-build-up from the entry. Evidently, atmosphere had the same deleterious effect on their beam-type weapons as it did to the Navy's.

Dogfighting in the Wasp was a hybrid melding of the pilot and the AI, in this case, Beth and Rose. Rose picked up deliberate and subconscious commands from the helmet pick-ups and calculated thrust and changes in the control surfaces to fight the *Tala* as Beth wanted. Without the helmet, Beth would have to actively fly the Wasp—with it, she almost *became* the *Tala*, thinking it through the flight, and that was a huge benefit when atmospheric flying.

A pilot in a dogfight had to take into account multiple and changing factors such as Angle of Attack, Angle Off Tail, Track Crossing Angle, the Velocity Vector, and a host of other considerations. Some only pertained to atmospheric flying. While most of their flying in the vacuum of space, Wasp pilots trained incessantly for atmospheric flight in both the cockpit and more often, in the sims to gain the almost instinctual skills needed to not only survive a mission, but to take out the enemy.

Beth didn't have to stop and consider any of these. She knew what she wanted to do, and her helmet interfaced with Rose and implemented it. She hadn't stopped to make a rational judgement on whether to put the *Tala* into a Split-S or an Immelmann turn—she simply knew that given the situation, an Immelmann would expose her to the bandit's weapons to a greater degree.

The enemy pilot had evidently trained, too. It pulled its fighter up to meet the *Tala* and hit her again, this time with the particle beam weapon. Beth pulled her fighter to the side, slipping out of the beam then jinking back again as the beam adjusted. She fired her own beamer on a broad pattern, not expecting to kill the bandit, but to make it pause as she maneuvered for position.

It worked. The bandit jinked as well, and Beth was in the clear.

Both fighters had closed to within 10 klicks, only 20,000 meters from the surface of the planet. Beth still had the altitude advantage, but she was diving while the bandit was climbing—climbing exceptionally fast. Beth was loath to give up that advantage, and she fired off another burst of her railgun as the two fighters passed each other, separated by a gut-churning 200 meters.

Incredibly, she evidently didn't hit the bandit—that or the enemy fighter was far more robust than anything the Navy had. She didn't want to admit that she missed the shot at such close range, but that was far more palatable than the second explanation.

She screamed to the planet surface, shooting the beamer to the rear to keep the enemy fighter from having free range. Her compensators whined and she pulled the *Tala* into an extremely tight turn, breaking at 1,000 meters over the ground at the bottom of her flight path, the *Tala* shuddering as it grabbed air.

A tiny section of her mind noted that Mercy had adjusted her course. That meant that she was alive, and she'd finally noticed what was going on. Beth wanted to shout out, but she had more on her mind, namely, an enemy fighter that had turned and was about to bear down on her from the advantage of altitude.

The bandit had climbed quicker than anything Beth had seen before—but that was because the Wasp had one advantage that she'd only experienced in a sim. In space, a pilot could enter G-Shock, and then boost the power of the Wasp, accelerating at 70+ G's. The *Tala's* FC engine had the highest mass-to-power ratio of any vessel known to humankind. It couldn't drive the *Tala* at 70 G's in an atmosphere and fighting a gravity well, but it would still give her a kick in the ass.

"Overide G-Shock," she said, enunciating clearly as the *Tala* rose to meet the threat, then when prompted, said, "One-four-one-nine-sierra-two."

"Overridden," Rose confirmed.

Beth wasn't sure exactly how hard she could push the *Tala*, and how long she could withstand it. She was already taking fire, and this time, her shields were depleting.

"Time to firewall," she said, locking her railgun onto the oncoming fighter. She tensed her stomach muscles as hard as she could, then gave Rose the command, grunting to keep from G-Lock.

It didn't work. She blacked out as the *Tala* shot forward.

Chapter 22

Beth came to, confused for a second. She'd been walking down a lighted tunnel one second, then she was strapped into her cockpit the next. It took her a moment to realize where she was.

Alarms were sounding, and she tried to make sense of what had just happened. The *Tala* was no longer accelerating, but she was back in the exosphere above Toowoomba and climbing quickly. First things first, so she started to slow the *Tala* down and bring her around.

She saw she'd been out for just four seconds. That wasn't much, but in a fighter, that might as well have been an hour. She had to find out what the situation was. She did a quick scan, and to her disappointment, the enemy fighter was still on her display. It wasn't chasing her, but it looked to be heading down to the planet's surface.

Panic hit her, and she checked on Mercy. To her relief, Mercy was still descending, almost on the ground, and the NSB-1 didn't seem to be chasing her. If it kept going on its present course, it would land near Mercy, but not on her.

That can change, of course, if the FAL adjusts its course.

One of her alarms was unfamiliar, and it took a moment to place it. It was a system breach alarm. Somewhere, the *Tala* had been breached. Beth ran a quick scan and saw that her canopy had been punctured.

She leaned forward, and sure enough, on the right side where the canopy retracted into the skin of the fighter, there was a 5-cm gap. She felt around the right edge of her seat opposite the gap, but she couldn't feel anything. Whatever had created the gap didn't look to have penetrated into the cockpit, but other than the fact that Beth hadn't been hit, it made little difference. Any break in the skin of a Wasp could have drastic consequences. The los of O2 could be the least of her problems.

She'd have to deal with that, but first, she had to figure out what was happening. She pulled up the bandit on her visuals. It didn't look to be in a controlled flight, but there was something else different about it. She recalled one of the earlier images and put it side-by-side. There was no question. A good chunk of the fighter was missing.

There were several ways to find out what happened, but the easiest was to recall on her display what had happened since she firewalled the *Tala*. A box opened up on the lower-left side of her display, inside which appeared the display from almost six minutes prior. As the *Tala* came around and started to descend again, Beth watched on her display as the image of her fighter surged forward. Her biologicals at the edge of the display indicated that she'd passed out almost immediately, and less than a second after that, as the two fighters closed, the railgun fired, sending 413 rounds in a single burst. The loss of integrity alarm sounded, and a few seconds later, as the sky turned to the darkness of space, Beth regained consciousness.

So, what happened to the bandit?

She couldn't tell from the general display, so she pulled up the targeting record. This was much better for her purposes. She could see the animation of the bandit, then the stream of depleted uranium rounds reach out to it. Incredibly, the enemy fighter jinked, and most of the rounds missed.

Most.

At least one, possibly two rounds tore into the side of the fighter, sending crystal shards flying. And that coincided with the cockpit breach. She'd answered two questions with this feed. She'd shot down the enemy fighter, but in doing so, she might have shot down herself. She'd passed so close to the bandit that she'd hit some of its debris. It evidently hadn't penetrated, but due to the combined closing speeds, it had been enough to crack her canopy.

And she was bleeding O2. Her tanks were still feeding it into the cockpit, and her scrubbers were probably still working, but with the hole in the canopy, it was escaping as soon as it was emitted. She needed to shut off the flow into the cockpit and rely solely on the feed to her helmet.

The *Tala* started to shudder again, but more violently than before. She was still high in the exosphere, and she wouldn't have thought there was that much of a partial pressure to rattle the fighter, but this was worse than before. Something else had to be wrong, but after a scan, she couldn't see anything.

She flipped her comms back on, trying to report in to Gollum. It was difficult to focus on the display through the vibrations, but she had the green link light lit. The problem was there was no answer. Either her comms were out, too, or the fight hadn't gone—

She cut off that train of thought. She would deal with the possibility that the two of them were the only survivors of the mission later. She had to figure out what to do now, and worrying about the rest would only interfere with that. It felt cold to her, but she knew she had to focus on what she could affect.

Assuming that Mercy's Wasp was inoperable, she could land near her and together, they could fit inside the *Tala*. She'd done it with Bull, after all, and he was much bigger than Mercy. Of course, that supposed many things, not the least was that the *Tala* would be operable. She had a hole in her canopy, for goodness sake. But if they could find some way to patch it, then it should be doable. They could get to the gate, and if was still open, they should be able to get back to secure space. If the gate were closed, then they'd have to wait with all the other human survivors for rescue.

The buffeting grew stronger, and Beth was thrown against her harness. She tried to flatten out the descent, but the Tala was responding sluggishly. Something definitely was wrong, and she couldn't see what it was. She glanced back to the gap in the canopy.

Oh, shit!

What had been a five-centimeter gap was now closer to ten. And she knew what was wrong, at least, what was causing the buffeting.

When she had been tested so long ago by Senior Chief Garcia, she'd felt the tiniest of imperfection along one of the vector ports. She'd refused to certify that Wasp and had passed the test. The reason that finding imperfections was important was that at high enough speeds, even the tiniest of imperfections could have drastic consequences. Beth was nowhere near the *Tala's* max speed now, but she was travelling blindingly fast for being in an atmosphere, and by descending, she was giving the air enough substance to grab at the *Tala* and tear her apart. She had to bring the fighter back up onto thinner air or the vacuum of space and slow down before trying to descend again—except, if she did that, she'd didn't know how much O2 she had.

I've got to chance it.

She started to give the command to turn back and gain altitude when with an explosive force, the canopy tore off, the wind slamming Beth with the force of a super-typhoon. Beth couldn't see anything, so violently was she being tossed around. Without the harness, she'd have been sucked out. With it, she was afraid of being torn in two.

Somehow, she managed to bend over, and the super-typhoon diminished to merely a Cat 5 storm. Her feet were relatively untouched, but the slipstream clawed at her back.

Oh, this is stupid, Floribeth. Don't do it.

She had to control the *Tala,* and she couldn't do that bent over or sitting upright, not with the canopy gone. She had to get lower into the cockpit.

Her harness had a retractable feature that would allow Beth limited mobility inside the cockpit. She activated it, then with a death grip on the bottom of her control panel, she pulled herself forward, fighting the slipstream. The wind's grip lessened ever so slightly as she got below the forward lip of the cockpit, right where the canopy had been only moments before. This was the moment of truth. The lungeline was at maximum extensions, and the wind was still unbelievably strong. Just a half a meter ahead of her, against the forward firewall, there was an eddy of calm. If she could reach it, she'd be safer. But that meant popping her harness, the only thing that had kept her in the *Tala* so far.

She was getting too beat up by the wind, and she didn't know how much she could take. With a damaged Wasp, she couldn't rely on it to get down to the planet's surface if she was unconscious.

She performed her fake cross kiss, then with one hand firmly grasping the rail on the bottom of her seat, she released the harness and pushed forward, jamming her body in the bottom of the cockpit, hugging the firewall.

She gasped for air—not for lack of O2, which was still being fed into her helmet, but from nerves. Nothing was keeping her inside the *Tala* except for gravity, and just centimeters from her, the wind was reaching into the cockpit with hurricane force. She was in a tiny eddy of almost still air.

"Mother of God," she whispered, surprised that she was still alive.

Now, to fly the *Tala*. With her canopy gone, so was her display. But her helmet had its own capabilities.

"Shift to helmet display," she ordered, going completely verbal.

There was no way she was going to reach up to activate any of the manual controls. Her helmet faceshield immediately lit up, giving her a miniaturized version of her full display. She had to bleed speed, and do it before she got into heavier air. She had enough O2 for several orbits, so she should have time and real estate in which to accomplish that.

Flying at high altitudes while not combat ready came with its own risks, however. Depending on what was going on out in the system, she could be making herself a "grape," or a pilot ripe for the plucking. She wished she knew what was happening out there, but she was flying blind to whatever was out beyond Toowoomba's atmosphere.

And then there was the minor fact that she had no canopy. If a small gap in the canopy had caused this catastrophic of an outcome, then in what would flying without one result?

She compromised. She'd do two orbits, bleeding as much speed as possible, before trying to descend again. If the *Tala* seemed to be holding together, she'd land near Mercy, and together they'd figure out their options.

With a sigh, she gave Rose the commands, then tried to hug the firewall to ride it out.

****

The wind was still too strong as the *Tala* approached the ground. Beth had tried to sit up to get a real view, but it had been too much for her, and she'd skootched back down to the bottom of the cockpit. She had a view from the feed, but she'd feel much better with real eyes seeing what was out there.

The last 35 minutes had been surreal. Scrunched up against the firewall, she had an inkling of how the monitor and other drone pilots did their thing. She felt removed from the *Tala*, not really there, as if she was controlling her from a distance. The big difference was that if she did make a big mistake, she was in her Wasp, and she'd suffer the physical consequences.

Among other things, her compensators were lost, so she felt each change of speed. Just as she spotted Mercy's Wasp on her feed, the *Tala* flared for a landing. Beth scrambled up and turned around, looking out over the bow of her fighter. Fifty meters ahead of her, the other fighter was basically whole, but it was obvious that it wasn't going to fly again, at least not without a complete overhaul. Half of the fighter was blackened, and it was cockeyed after one of the landing struts had collapsed. There was no sign of Mercy.

After such a rough ride, the *Tala* settled down with barely a bump. Beth removed her M-20 from the cockpit holster, checked the load, and carefully surveyed the scene before climbing down and onto the ground.

First time I've done this, she noted offhand.

For all of her now 58 missions, she'd never set foot on a target planet.

There was no movement around Mercy's Wasp. The canopy was closed and darkened, and she couldn't see in. Feeling dread in her heart for what she was about to find, Beth slowly walked forward, M-20 pointed ahead.

"Mercy? Are you there?" she asked as she came closer to the Wasp.

There was no answer.

"Mercy?"

The tang of ionized air stung her nostrils as she reached the fighter. Hesitantly, she reached forward with the little M-20, tapping the canopy with the barrel. There was no reaction.

And there was no getting around what she had to do next. She depressed the emergency access panel, then turned the small red lever. The canopy cracked, and Beth reached over and pulled it back into its recess, waiting to see the worst.

It was empty.

There was a rush of noise from behind her, and Beth spun around, her M-20 ready to fire when a body slammed into her.

"I just knew that was you up there, Beth, but why? Why did you risk that? And why are you here now?" Mercy sobbed, holding Beth in a death grip.

Beth slowly pushed Mercy away so she could look into her face.

"Because you're my wingman, sista. Of course, I was coming," she told her as tears rolled down her face as well.

Chapter 23

"Nothing?" Beth asked.

"Not a fucking thing," Mercy answered, pulling back from where she'd been leaning in the *Tala's* cockpit. "Not that I know what the hell I'm doing."

"It's just switching out the modules. It was worth a try, though."

The comms on both Wasps were down—hard down. It wasn't because there was no one out there to hear them, although as much as they didn't want to dwell on it, that could be the case. Neither one of the two comms suites was transmitting. The two friends had decided that they could try to switch out the control modules, first taking the *Tala's* to Mercy's Wasp, and when that didn't work, taking Mercy's to the *Tala*.

Mercy climbed back down, module in hand. She turned it over in her hand as if she could see why it didn't work, then dropped it, forgotten, in the dirt.

"So, now what?" she asked. "Any other ideas?"

Beth hesitated, turning to look over her shoulder before asking, "You said the FAL came down over in that direction?"

"Yeah. So?"

"And not too far?"

"Not too far. I mean, I saw it, so it couldn't have been. I wasn't sure what it was, FAL or one of us."

"It's got to be them," Beth said. "No one else was coming here."

"Not that you know of. Why do you ask, anyway?"

Beth hadn't completely formed a plan yet. She was positive that the NSB-1 had wanted to get Mercy's Wasp intact. Maybe Mercy along in the bargain. This would have given them an advantage in their fight with humanity.

But the same would hold true with humans getting a hold one of their ships as well. Rumor was that some capital ships were being modified for a snatch and grab job, to just that end. But to date, all the humans had was the remains of a torpedo and some ship fragments.

"I think we should go check it out," she said.

"What, the crash site?"

"Yeah, the crash site."

"Like, on foot? Walk there?"

"We sure can't fly," Beth said, nodding at the two grounded Wasps.

"Don't you remember your classes back at flight school? If you go down, stay with your birds. That's how SAR finds you."

"And in SERE, you have to get away from your ride. That's how the enemy finds you."

"But this is a human planet. We want to be found," Mercy said.

"It was a human planet. We don't know what it is now."

Mercy shrugged, then said, "I don't think much of anything is left. It came in hard, and I heard the boom when it hit. Nothing could have survived that."

"I don't know. I hit it with my railgun, and it still made it down here. I think they're pretty tough. Besides, even if it's destroyed, remember how excited the eggheads were with the torpedo fragments?"

Mercy toed the dirt, making a line, then brushing it away before saying, "Maybe."

"Come on, let's go see. We can take a look, then leave, but at least we'll know enough to file a report."

Mercy was an NSP2 while Beth was an NSP3. Given military protocol, Mercy was now in charge.

"We can set the self-destruct on a timer. If we don't get back, then they'll blow."

"Don't get back, Beth? Fuck, you really know how to convince a girl."

"I think it's our duty," Beth said quietly.

"I know, I know. It's just that, I didn't think I'd make it, and then, it's like I was given a new leaf on life. So . . ."

Beth stayed quiet. She knew what Mercy would decide, but she had to come to the decision herself.

It only took a moment.

"Fuck it. I'm living on borrowed time now, right?"

Mercy walked back to her Wasp, reached inside, and pulled out her M-20 before returning to Beth.

"You remember how to use this thing?"

"We had to fire them at flight school," Beth said.

"Yeah, but I wasn't paying any attention. I just let the range NCO set it up for me, and I pulled the trigger." She looked at it, turning it over, then asked, "Isn't there some kind of safety on it?"

"That's for range weapons. This is yours. Your hand is the safety."

"Oh, yeah," she said, still not looking sure of herself.

"Give me it," Beth said, holding her hand out.

She checked to make sure the magazine was seated, then chambered a round, and then handed it back to Mercy.

"There. You're ready."

The M-20 was a heavy-caliber slug thrower. Almost fool-proof, it was pretty accurate out to 25 meters, and it would stop a person pretty much no matter where it hit them. More than that, it was extremely robust. At the range, one had been put into a flaming barrel for 15 minutes, then pulled out and fired. Beth was no expert with it, but she was pretty sure she could hit a person—or an FAL—if the need arose.

They set the self-destructs for six hours, then started off in the direction that Mercy had seen the NSB-1 ship come down. They started out slowly, carefully placing their feet so as to minimize noise as Marines did in the holovids, but that took a lot of effort. Five minutes in, they both started to relax, and within ten, they were walking side-by-side as if on a stroll though a city park.

"Think there'll be anything there?" Mercy asked.

"Something. The science types can get a lot of info from just traces."

"This isn't Gee-Eff-Eye," Mercy said.

GFI was Galactic Forensic Investigators, a crime/romance drama where the married forensic investigators could solve any crime with the tiniest piece of information. More romance than science, it was quite popular.

"No, but I'm betting there'll be enough for analysis."

Toowoomba was a pretty planet, at least here, and they walked in silence for awhile, grateful for the pleasant weather. Humankind occupied many worlds, and not all were comfortable places to be.

"Beth . . ."

"Yes?"

"About your brother . . ."

Beth held up her hand, palm out, to stop her, but she continued, blurting out, "I just want you to know that I'm not fooling around. I really like him."

"And if my mother and I asked you not to communicate with him anymore?"

Mercy stopped, and the coldness came rushing back like an arctic wind.

"I love you, Beth, but I'd still see him."

Beth stopped and looked at her for a long moment before saying, "I know you care for him, but even if you didn't, I was out of line. What you and he do is between the two of you, not me."

"Really? I . . . are you sure? Because we are going to see each other again," she said.

"I know you are. He told me as much." She stepped up and put her hands on Mercy's upper arms and looked deep into those brown eyes, then said, "Whatever else happens, you make him happy."

"I do?" she said, a note of . . . hope?. . . in her voice.

"You do. And he deserves that." Beth pulled Mercy in to a hug. "I'm sorry it took me so long to say that, and I'm sorry we've been . . ." she trailed off.

"I'm sorry, too."

Standing there on a planet under siege, on their way to see what was left of an alien spacecraft, the two stood hugging, and more than a few tears fell.

"Damn! Sorry for the waterworks," Mercy said, finally pushing back and wiping the tears. "Look at us. Not very Navy-like, huh? Let's get back on the job and go see what's left of the fucking FAL you splashed."

Beth wiped her own tears and nodded, and said, "That's redundant, you know."

"What?"

"'Fucking FAL.' That means 'Fucking fucking alien.'"

"Leave it to you to point that out," Mercy said, shaking her head in mock exasperation.

"I know you missed that part of me lately," Beth said as the two stepped off again.

Despite having a wrecked Wasp, despite being marooned on another planet, and despite not knowing what had happened with the rest of the squadron in the battle, Beth felt better right then than she had felt in a long time.

Within half an hour, they knew they were getting close. They could smell it. There was a burned vegetation smell, one Beth knew well from New Cebu, but there was something else, something that burned their noses.

"Look at that," Mercy said, toeing what looked to be a 20 kg chunk of black crystal.

Both of them stood there for a moment. That had to have come from the NSB-1 craft. It had been made by an alien life form, probably in the Perseus Arm, and here it was, at their feet, just another piece of space junk.

"Mark the spot," Mercy said. "If nothing else, we can haul this back with us."

The two slowed back down for a more cautious approach. The acrid smell got stronger, and they found more pieces of broken craft scattered on the ground.

"There it is," Beth said, catching sight of a black and deep grey object through the smashed trees.

They slowed down even further, watching their feet as they crept closer. The alien ship—and that was what it had to be—was a mass of crystals, all sticking out and odd angles. Some had obviously been shorn off as it crashed. About the size of three Wasps, Beth was amazed that much was still whole given the length and depth of the furrow in the ground and the number of smashed trees that littered the area. She wondered how much of the ship had been taken off when she hit it with her railgun.

"That's never going to fly again," Mercy said in a hushed voice.

If looking at the shard behind them had given them pause, then this was awe-inspiring. Looking nothing like any ship known to humankind, it had transported the enemy alien here to Toowoomba.

"Think it's in there?" Beth asked.

"Only one way to find out," Mercy answered, then stepped out from the cover of the trees.

"Shit, Mercy," Beth muttered as she hurried after her, M-20 at the ready as she scanned the area.

There were slight pings and pops as they approached the downed ship, possibly from cooling, Beth thought. The aliens seemed to like heat weapons, so their ships had to have methods for dealing with them from a defensive posture.

"So, where's the cockpit," Mercy asked, standing two meters from the ship, hands on her hips.

Beth didn't have an answer for that. There was nothing about the mass of crystals that hinted at a cockpit, controls, or anything she could attribute to a space-going vessel.

Mercy held out a hand to touch it, and Beth knocked it down.

"We don't know what it is, Mercy."

Mercy shrugged, then looked around her feet, bending down to pick up a small leafy branch that had broken off a bush or tree. She held it out and touched the leaves to the crystal side of the ship. Beth held her breath, afraid of what might happen, but curious as well.

Nothing happened. The leaves were still the leaves, the branch was still the branch. Mercy dropped it, and before Beth could say anything, she reached out and touched the side.

"Oh, wow," she said, right before suddenly jerking upright into a rigid posture, mouth open before toppling over backward.

"Mercy!" Beth screamed, dropping to her knees beside her and shaking her shoulder. "Wake up, wake up!"

Mercy, slowly turned her head to Beth, eyes wide open, before she broke out into laughter and said, "Sorry, I couldn't help myself. You should have seen your face!"

"What? You . . . you . . . fuck you, Mercy Hamlin! That wasn't funny!" Beth screamed, punching her in the upper arm.

"Yeah, it was, Floribeth Salinas O'Shae Dalisay," Mercy said, getting back up to her feet and rubbing her arm.

"You scared the shit out of me."

"That was the whole point of it," Mercy said, stepping back up to the ship. "'Fucking fucking aliens' my ass."

She reached out again, placing her hand back on the ship.

"It's vibrating."

Beth was still breathing heavily, still in shock, and still upset, but curiosity was getting the better of her.

"Vibrating?"

"Yeah, feel it."

She hesitated only a second, then placed her hand flat on the nearest facet. It was vibrating, very slightly, but without question.

"It almost as if it's alive," Beth said. "Do you think this is the FAL? I mean, there's not some alien inside of it, but the ship itself, could it be the alien?

Mercy turned her head to look at her, and in unison, both women whipped their hands off the ship.

"Oh, I don't know," Mercy said. "Do you think?"

"I don't know what to think. But we've got to get this location to our forces. Let them come figure it out."

"Look at that," Mercy said, pointing.

Beth turned her head. The crystal formation jutting out just over their heads had been snapped off. In the middle of the sheared edge, a new crystal had formed and was pushing out, obviously since the original shard had been broken off.

"It's growing," Mercy said.

Beth thought she was right. It had to be growing. And that meant the ship was repairing itself. That led to the possibility that the ship could somehow leave the planet's surface before humankind could salvage it.

"No!" she shouted, then said, "We've got to get our forces here. Did you see how far the processing station was?"

"About 21 klicks that way," Mercy said.

"We're going to have to run it, then hope there's something there."

"I swore I'd never run again after boot camp," Mercy muttered, and before Beth could light into her, she added, "But I've sworn off a lot of things that I keep doing. One more won't hurt."

"OK, let's go," Beth said. "The sooner we get there, the longer the Navy will have to come get this thing before it flies away on us."

They had just stepped away from the ship when a clicking sound reached them from the trees on the other side of the ship. Beth looked over her shoulder just as she broke into a jog, then stopped dead, grabbing Mercy's shoulder to stop her, too.

"What the fuck?" Mercy asked.

Coming out from the trees, 40 meters away, was a smaller version of the ship—no not really a version of it. It was smaller, and it was made of some crystalized structure, but it had a more lifelike sense about it. Beth instinctively knew this was the alien itself, not the ship, and she brought her M-20 to bear.

In the scifi holovids, aliens almost always had discernable heads, legs, and arms or tentacles. Not so this thing. It was as if a mineral deposit had come to life. Beth couldn't even tell how it was moving, but moving it was, and right at them.

She fired three rounds from her M-20, and she could see at least two of them glance off the thing, not slowing it down in the least.

"Shoot, Mercy!" she shouted as the alien closed the distance.

Beside her, Mercy fired twice while Beth fired three more rounds. A tiny crystal tine on the alien exploded into a black mist, but that was all. The clicking sound increased in frequency.

She fired another round, hitting the thing straight on, but once again, with no effect. The FAL was coming at them, and it didn't look like their M-20s were going to do them any good. They could keep firing until it bowled into them in a few seconds, or they could . . .

"Run!" Beth shouted.

She bolted to the right while Mercy bolted to the left. The alien shifted its approach to head towards Mercy, and Beth fired another shot as she ran in a futile attempt to distract it.

Looking back in horror, she saw the alien lower a crystal tine, and a white web shot out at Mercy, part of it hitting her shoulder and back. Whatever it was, it seemed to fold around her, making her stumble to her knees.

"Mercy!" Beth screamed, coming to a halt.

Mercy tried to get back up, but like a malevolent lace shawl from a horror holovid, the white thing continued to expand its grip on her. Mercy dropped her M-20, struggled to take two steps before she became too entangled and fell face-first to the ground.

The alien slowed down to almost a crawl as it moved to her, completely ignoring Beth. For a moment, she thought Mercy was dead, and anger flowed through her as she started to run at it. To do what, well, she hadn't figured that out yet.

And then she stopped dead in her tracks, 15 meters behind the hulking thing. Mercy wasn't dead. The thing was impervious to their little handguns, and it was much bigger than either of them. She was absolutely sure that if it had wanted to kill them, it could, just as it could have blown Mercy out of the sky.

No, Mercy wasn't dead—she was a prisoner. The alien wanted a human captive to take back for their NSB-1 versions of scientists. They wanted to find out what made humans tick so they could more efficiently kill them.

"Ain't gonna happen," Beth muttered.

She had no idea why the thing was ignoring her. Maybe it only focused on one thing at a time. Beth had often been ignored due to her diminutive size, so this was nothing new to her. People often regretted being dismissive of her, so she had to make sure this hunk of crystals would regret it, too.

But how? The thing had to weigh 300 kgs to Beth's 32. Her M-20 wasn't having any effect on it.

Maybe if I fire at point-blank range? Right in the middle of it?

It was worth a try. The alien had reached Mercy and was standing still, as if studying its prize. Or maybe gloating. Beth knew she wouldn't be ignored forever, so she had to act now. Trying to think herself smaller than she was, she quietly approached it from what she hoped was the back. For all she knew, it could see in all directions, but she didn't have many options.

She was still five meters away, looking for a likely target on the thing when it shot out another white net, this time keeping one end attached, the other end connecting to the white lace on Mercy. Beth froze in place, but the thing still seemed oblivious to her presence, and it started to move again, dragging Mercy towards the ship. Beth had a quick glimpse of Mercy's panic-filled eyes looking back at her.

The time for trying to sneak up on the thing was over. If it managed to get Mercy inside that ship, then Beth knew it was over. She had to act now.

She ran the last few steps and raised her M-20, ready to shoot into the center of the thing when she noticed something different about a section on it. Most of it was made out of the crystal substance, the stuff that seemed impervious to her handgun. But there was a 20-centimeter tube-like structure that protruded out of a gray crystal box and into the main chunk of alien. She had no idea what it was, but it wasn't crystal. Without even thinking, she took aim, and just as the alien started to turn as if finally noticing her, she fired two rounds. One ricocheted off the box, but the other cut the tube clean in two.

The reactions were, well, impressive.

Green gas shot out from the tube, a vile, burning gas that made Beth recoil and dive out of the way—where she was almost crushed by the whirling dervish the alien had become. She scrambled back on her butt, trying to put more distance between her and the thing as it writhed and jerked, crystal tines going crazy as the clicking got much, much louder. Green gas kept escaping from the broken end of the tube on the gray box side.

Suddenly, the alien darted towards the ship, dragging Mercy with it until it dropped its hold on the white lace-thing it had used to pull her. It reached the ship and crashed full force into the side, bouncing back a good three meters, then rushing it again, this time hitting it with less force.

Beth watched all this in awe. Whatever she'd hoped to accomplish, this scenario hadn't been it.

The quivering alien raised two larger structures and touched the ship. The structures seemed to meld into the ship, and Beth jumped up and started to run at it. It was trying to get into the ship, and she was positive that would give it sanctuary from whatever peril it was in. It may have been trying to capture Mercy, but it would be pretty pissed off, and if they were anything like humans, revenge would be on its mind. Beth didn't want to give it the opportunity to extract that revenge.

She ran up to it, ready to fire her remaining rounds at it, but the shaking had diminished to a few quivers, then they ceased altogether. The clicking stopped, too. With a sharp ping that made Beth jump, the two arm structures detached from the ship and drifted down.

The Fucking Alien was dead.

Beth stood on her tiptoes and touched the broken tube. It was soft and had give. Green was still coming out of the box

So, the scientists were right. They are chlorine breathers.

Nothing was coming out of the other broken end of the tube. Something had gone in, though. O2. Great for humans, not so much for something that breathed chlorine. Beth idly wondered if the thing had suffocated or been poisoned.

She felt weird. Maybe it had been a whiff of the chlorine, but probably she was coming down from the battle high. Either way, she didn't seem connected to reality at the moment, as if she was merely watching a holovid.

"Hey, a little help here?" Mercy cried out.

Shit, yeah, Mercy.

She walked over to where Mercy was lying, trussed up in white lace.

"Hmph," Beth snorted, trying to figure out what to do.

"Don't you fucking 'hmph' me. Get me out of here."

"I don't know. Are you playing around again?" Beth asked, feeling giddy from killing the alien and more than willing to make her friend suffer from scaring her before.

"Quit fucking around and get me out of here!"

She took pity on her friend and pulled out her survival knife, kneeling beside her. Knife raised, she hesitated. For all she knew, the stuff holding Mercy was uncuttable, or that by cutting it, it could react in a deleterious way, maybe by constricting.

Suddenly serious, she thought that maybe they'd better wait until they had some help.

"Hurry, Beth," Mercy said, her voice plaintive.

"I'm not sure that's a good idea. What if that thing reacts?"

"I don't care, just do it. I'm freaking out."

Beth shook her head, then slipped the point of her blade below a strand of lace and pulled up. To her surprise, the lace readily parted. She cut more, and within twenty seconds, a very relieved Mercy kicked herself free. She jumped to her feet and did a half shudder, half dance that pushed Beth over the edge. She just stood and laughed, reaching to take the surprised Mercy's hands in hers and doing her own little dance.

Mercy pulled her in for a hug, stopping the dance.

"I knew I was a goner, Beth. But I forgot about you. I should have known you had my six," she whispered in her ear.

"You'd have done the same for me."

"I would have tried, sista. But could I have managed it? You killed that big motherfucker," she said, breaking the hug and looking over at the dead alien.

"Yeah, it's dead. We were lucky. But luck or not, we're alive, Mercy, we're alive."

****

"You two there, hands up!" a voice called out.

"Really?" Mercy muttered, then yelled out, "We're fucking humans!"

"That don't look like nothing human," the voice said. "So, until we know what you are, hands up, or by God, we'll shoot you first, then figure out what you are later."

"Just get up," Beth told Mercy as she stood, hands in the air.

"They don't know who they're dealing with," Mercy said, but she did stand.

A moment later, two men and three women stepped out into the clearing made when the NSB-1 ship crashed. They were in bright orange work overalls, and the way they kept staring at the ship instead of the two pilots left little doubt that these were civilians workers and not military.

They had real guns, though, and being civilians, they might be nervous and more trigger-happy.

"Who are you," the oldest-looking women said.

"We're in Navy flight suits, so doesn't that answer your question?" Mercy said.

"Don't give me your shit. I want an answer."

"I'm NSP3 Floribeth Dalisay. This is NSP2 Mercy Hamlin. We're Navy pilots who were shot down in the battle with the NSB-1s."

"Then where are your ships?" one of the men asked. "That ain't no Navy ship. I know that. And what the hell's an NSB-1?""

"Our ships are back there," Mercy said, keeping her hands up, but rotating a wrist in the general direction. "And an NSB-1 is an alien species that has attacked humanity. That there is its ship. The lump beside it is the alien pilot."

All of this was highly classified, Beth knew, but they could see the thing there.

The five exchanged looks, and the second man said, "I knew it. I just knew it."

"Uh, can we lower our arms now?" Mercy asked.

The woman nodded, but the first man objected, saying, "Hona, we still don't know who they are. They can be shapeshifters or such."

"Give it a break, Dave. They're human, and Navy at that. We need to help them."

"But—"

"No buts."

"Thank you," Beth said as she lowered her arms. "Uh . . . can you tell us what happened up there? In the battle?"

"We don't have all the details. The attackers . . . I guess they really were aliens," she said, "wiped out most of Innamincka. Maybe a million dead. Maybe less. We don't know. Down here, nothing."

She seemed lost in thought. Beth could understand that. A million dead was almost too difficult to comprehend. But she had to know what the status was now.

"What about the battle? With the Navy?"

"Oh, that. You folks won, I guess. They're up there now at least, and the fighting's stopped."

Beth felt a wave of relief sweep through her, then some guilt for that considering the massive loss of life aboard the station.

"No one much is talking to us now. Told us to stay in place until further notice, but we saw that thing, I'm guessing, come out of the sky, so we decided to take a look. Heard your shooting fifteen minutes ago, so we hurried to get here quicker."

"Do you have any communications that I can use? We need to reach our command."

"They've opened up an emergency net. I don't know if that'll work. We can patch you through the refinery."

"That'll do," Mercy said. "Can we get access to it?"

"Dave, give them your set."

"But—"

"Damn it, Dave, just do it."

"Yeah, just do it, Dave," Mercy said.

Dave shook his head, then called up the refinery and asked to be patched through to the emergency net. Mercy stepped up, hand out, and he started a little stare-down with Mercy, then pointedly handed it to Beth. It took her five minutes of explaining who she was and getting routed, but she eventually was connected with Commander Tuominen, somewhere up there in his Wasp.

"Fire Ant, thank God. What is your situation now? We've got your Wasps' location, but no connectivity."

"Both Wasps are down hard and cannot fly. We're fine. What's the situation up there?" she asked.

She didn't have a need to know, but she was anxious to know what had happened.

"You're reminded that this is not a secure net. But . . . we have the situation 95% contained."

So, the fight isn't over, but the situation is well in hand, she thought, translating what the commander had said.

"I need you to stay put for now. When the situation allows for it, SAR will come and pick you two up."

"That's a negative."

"What?" he asked, the first time Beth had ever heard him sound confused.

A SAR had room to pick up four, possible five people in a pinch. It could not carry cargo.

"We are not with our fighters. We are approximately 12 klicks to the south-south-east. You should be able to find us."

"OK, we can route the SAR to you."

"Negative. No SAR. You need to send a salvage tug," she said, looking over at the alien ship. "Something big enough to pick up a Badger-class shuttle."

There was dead silence on the other side of the line, then the commander said, "I am not understanding you, Fire Ant."

Beth was pretty sure that the big secret was about to get out, but this was still an unsecure line, so she shouldn't be giving too many details. It wasn't up to her to break the story.

"Red Devil and I have got something here," she said as Mercy reached over to fist bump her, a huge smile almost cracking her face open, "that our friends at home are going to want to see.

"I respectfully request that you get that salvage tug here ASAP, highest priority."

There was another pause, longer this time, then the commander said, "It's being done. Wait there and stand by on the comms."

"Sorry, I've got to keep this for now," she told Dave.

He accepted that with a nod. He and the second woman dropped their backpacks and rested their weapons on them, looking to settle in to wait.

Hona seemed unsure of herself, and she asked, "Now what? This is getting pretty intense. Do we need to leave?"

If Beth asked, she knew she'd be told to get the civilians out of there. The still unnamed second woman started rummaging her pack, pulling out some drink packs and handing them out.

Beth looked at Mercy, who shrugged, then accepted an Indigo from the woman with the drinks.

The woman looked at her, held out another Indigo, and asked, "You want something?"

"Yeah, if you've got a Coke in there," she said facetiously.

The woman put the Indigo back in the pack, and unbelievably, pulled out a familiar red pack and tossed it to Beth, who snatched it out of the air. She flipped the cooling tab, and ten seconds later, took a long, very much appreciated, swallow.

"You didn't answer me. Do we need to leave?" Hona asked.

Beth took another swallow, then said, "This is history in the making here, Hona. If you want to be part of it, more than you already are, I mean, just sit back, and relax."

EARTH

Chapter 24

"So, what do you think?" Commander Tuominen asked.

"I could get used to it," Mercy answered.

Beth didn't say anything. The cost of this meal could feed her village for a week. She felt guilty for eating it, despite how delicious it was, but she also felt special. She couldn't believe that she could ever have emerged out of New Cebu to come here to Earth itself and dine at Torreror's, one of the finest restaurants in the galaxy. Mercy's family had money, but this was even beyond her reach.

Working with the commander, she sometimes forgot how the GT's lived. He was almost more alien to her than the crystals.

The last three weeks had been hectic. She'd been correct back there on Toowoomba, waiting for the salvage tug. The secret was no more. The directorate may have wanted to keep it so, but that genie wasn't going back into the bag. They did take a week to decide how to break the news.

The fight in the Toowoomba system had been brutal. Hona hadn't been correct as to the human casualties. "Only" a little over 200,000 people had lost their lives, but that was still an immense number, more lives lost in a single incident for almost 30 years. The reported number was even lower at 42,116. Beth didn't know how the government would get away with underreporting like that, but that wasn't her concern.

The battle between the crystals—no more "FALs," which had only been used by the squadron. Some media wonk had used the term "crystals," and that had taken over the lexicon—had been accurately reported by the Navy, however. Twenty-two Wasps had been taken out of the fight, and fifteen pilots had been lost. Beth mourned them every single day since then. Fifteen friends, fifteen comrades. Hurl, who had become like a little brother to her, had been among the number.

Thirty-five crystal ships had been destroyed, six had escaped—and one was captured. Mercy and Beth, along with the commander, had become the face of the squadron. The three ranged from the social status of humanity: a GT, a wealthy but "regular" person, and one of the teeming masses struggling to make ends meet. The media moguls could not have cast them better.

Between their real debriefs by the Navy, interviews with the media, and meetings with the movers and shakers here on Earth, Beth hadn't even been able to sit down and digest things, to get a grasp on what had happened.

At least this was their last night on their whirlwind tour. To celebrate, the commander had taken them to Torreror's. And Tol himself had welcomed them to their table, treating the commander like an old friend. Even for a GT, that was impressive. Beth knew, of course, that the Tuominen family was one of the most powerful in humanity, but with him serving in the Navy, she'd just assumed he was from one of the offshoot branches. Now, she was not so sure.

Tomorrow, they were heading back to Sierra Station, and hopefully, back to reality. As much as she appreciated what she'd experienced, she wanted normality again. She was a pilot, not a media op for every politician who had enough pull to meet them.

Lost in her thoughts, she didn't notice a little girl, maybe five years old, and dressed in the cutest pink pantalet and matching blouse, who walked up to them, full of confidence. Behind her, an embarrassed looking woman followed apologetically.

"Mz. Fire Ant, I'm Stacilyn. May I please get an autograph?" she said, carefully enunciating each word.

"I'm so sorry," the woman said. "I don't want to bother you, but she insisted."

"No problem," Beth answered the woman, then turned to the girl and said, "I'd be honored. Come here and sit in my lap, if you want."

A smile broke out over her face, and she clambered up into Beth's lap.

"She's almost as big as you are," Mercy said with an affectionate smile.

"OK, smile," the girl's mother, Beth assumed, took the shot.

She handed it to Beth, who quickly signed the pad. A moment later, her signature appeared on the image display.

Stacilyn held it for a moment, then turned and said, "Thank you!"

"Can I have a copy?" Beth asked.

The little girl turned to her mother, who nodded. Beth entered her address, then let the girl hit the send.

"Thank you, Stacilyn. What about Mercy? You can get her autograph, too, you know."

"That's OK. You're my favorite," she said before sliding off Beth's knee and running to her mother to show her the autograph.

Beth looked up at Mercy in horror, but her friend just laughed it off. She'd had a few too many drinks and was in a happy place.

"Do you know who that was?" the commander asked.

"Her name is Stacilyn."

"No, the woman."

"No, sir."

The restaurant was priced so high that only the movers and shakers would be there, so the woman was undoubtedly rich, but other than that, she didn't know her at all.

"Krisana Albescu."

Beth looked up in surprise at the woman, just now sitting back down at her table while Stacilyn showed the rest of the table her new autograph. Beth had heard of the Rose Assassin, of course. Everyone had heard of her. She was one of the most powerful norms in all of humankind, famous for destroying her business rivals, then taking over their ruined businesses at decas to the BC. She looked way too young to be who she was, but then again, the best mods money can buy probably went a long way to achieve that look.

People either loved or hated her, and among the people of New Cebu, that leaned towards the love. Beth was tempted to go over there right now and get an autograph of her own. Her ina would get a huge kick out of that.

These last few weeks had been surreal, to say the least, but as they left the restaurant, with a bag of "late night snacks" personally prepared by An Tol, Beth was glad it was almost over. It would be good to get back into the cockpit and have things go back to normal.

DS VICTORY

Chapter 25

Something dug into her side, and Beth came to, wondering for a moment just where she was.

"Wake up, Sleeping Beauty," Mercy whispered out of the corner of her mouth.

Oh, hell. Did anyone see?

There were at least five thousand people gathered in Hangar D. Yes, someone saw. And if any of them had missed it, several billion were supposedly watching from around human space.

How could you fall asleep, Floribeth?

Staying up for the last two days was probably a good reason, but having the director himself drone on certainly was a factor as well. He had to know that his speech was going to go down in history, and he seemed damned sure that he was going to make those historians work. He'd been going on for close to 40 minutes now, hitting every beat necessary to both identify the threat, then rally humankind to meet it.

Beth had met the man three times now, and she wasn't quite sure what she made of him yet. He was certainly an able executive, but there was something about him that didn't sit right.

Yeah, and you're the one to pass judgement on him. You're just a dumb fighter jock, Floribeth, so just smile and act like you're interested.

It was hard, though. The man just wouldn't shut up, but sitting one behind him and just off to his right, she had to at least look the part. She stole a little glance at the man sitting to her left. If someone could sit at attention, the Marine colonel was doing so, and she didn't think he'd moved a centimeter in all that time.

The man looked hard. That was probably good for the commanding officer of the ground force, but he kind of scared her.

She straightened up her posture, and the Platinum Star shifted across her breast. She was acutely aware of its heft, but she didn't look down. She'd earned the first one almost eight months ago, but it was only today, as she was awarded a second, that she was now authorized to wear it and her Silver Star.

Mercy had hers, too, but there was a difference. Beth's first award rated the "egg-beater," the propellers denoting that the award was earned in the cockpit, just the same as Mercy's Gold Star. This time, both she and Mercy were given the Platinum Star with the crossed swords attachment, to denote earning it in ground combat. The admiral had told her that he couldn't find any case where someone had earned Platinum Stars with both devices. He joked that he should send her to one of the capital ships so she could earn the fouled anchor for a clean sweep.

A capital ship like this one, she suddenly realized.

The *Victory* was decked out in a festive manner. For the masses, this was the start of taking the war to the crystals. This entire ceremony was for public consumption. First, the five Platinum Stars awarded: to Mercy, her, and three fellow pilots. Then, the Orders of Honor finally publicly given to Swordfish and Tuna, as well as to a Space Guard pilot who'd managed to splash one of the crystals in defense of

Innamincka Station. Then came the speeches, the director being the sixth, but most long-winded.

Of course, the war had been underway for months now. Just yesterday, the newly formed VFX-21, stationed with Third Fleet, had popped their battle cherry as a unit. The release to the public, however, was being tightly controlled so as not to induce panic, but still impart the seriousness of the situation.

And nothing gave confidence like showing off "heroes," but more than that, putting on a military parade. And if you were going to put on a parade, you couldn't do much better than show off a battle carrier task force.

The dignitaries were seated in a set of metal bleachers in three rows, right up against the hangar curtain, facing inboard to where the guests were seated in folding chairs. Behind the dignitaries and outside the ship, but in full view, were six Wasps, held steady in tractor beams. Behind them stretched the eight ships of the soon to be commissioned Task Force Iron Shield.

Inside the hangar, split into two groups and standing at attention on either side of the guests, were almost 2000 Marines in full combat armor. Beth didn't envy them. At least she had a seat.

Of course, none of them just fell asleep, she reminded herself ruefully.

Finally, the director wound down. Beth thought he looked pleased with himself. Frankly, she didn't know if it was a good speech or not, and she was just glad it was over.

There was one item left: the commissioning.

The director started to sit back down until an aide quickly intercepted him and sent him back to the podium where Rear Admiral Glorious Nzama stood waiting. The *Victory's* CO was Captain Whitehorse, a pilot, but the overall command of the task force went to the admiral, a swabbie who'd commanded every class of ship from a Rapier on up.

Beth knew next to nothing about swabbies, nor of shipboard life, so this was going to be interesting.

She stood facing the director while a voice read the order establishing the task force. It was mercifully brief. A lieutenant commander with a gold braid around his shoulder stepped up with a furled set of colors and handed them to the director, then pulled off the cover. The blue flag fell free, the Navy of Humankind's emblem in the center, "Task Force 39" above, and "Iron Shield" below.

The admiral took the colors almost reverently, then turned to face the guests. With a smile on her face, she started waving the flag to a standing ovation.

Beth stood and applauded, too. She'd been bored to death during the speeches, but this was different. She was caught up in the drama, and she felt a part of something far bigger than she was.

The admiral waved the colors for half-a-minute before stopping and handing it back to the lieutenant commander. She shook hands with the director, and just like that, the ceremony was over.

Task Force Iron Shield was ready for combat.

"Well, that's it," Mercy said. "Let's make sure our rides are OK. These dipwad greenshirts will probably fuck them up, and I don't want *Louhi* scratched."

Both of them had received the brand new FX-6M's to replace their lost Wasps, and as some of the newest fighters, they had been among the six to be used as displays. Mercy had never named her last Wasp, but when the new one arrived, she said it deserved a name. She'd chosen "Louhi," for some bad ass Finnish goddess.

People were leaving the bleachers. Most of the ones sitting would be at the reception in the admiral's mess, including Mercy and her, but the rest would be loaded up on the shuttles and taken across to Charlie Station. The *Victory* was too big to use the station gates, so this was going to take some time.

As she stepped down, she jostled the colonel. He looked down at her chest, and for a moment she bristled until she realized that he was looking a little higher than many men might look, right at her medal. He had a Silver Star, but nothing higher, and she realized that the big bad Marine was more than a little impressed with her hardware, especially with the crossed swords attachment.

She puffed up her chest and ignored his stare, but reveled in it all the same. She knew that was probably petty, but she never claimed to be perfect.

The two made their way to the roped off area where the six Wasps would be brought in. They ducked under the rope.

"I'm sorry, but you're going to have to . . . the greenshirt started before he saw who they were. "Oh, OK. You're fine."

The first Wasp came in, floating like a feather. It landed on the apron, and the canopy retracted. A smiling AT3 Joshua Frye stuck his head out. Some day, she was going to take him out in a two-seater recon version, but for now, sitting in it while the ship's tractor beam maneuvered it was going to have to do.

The Foxtrot model looked no different from the outside, but it had some serious upgrades on the inside, and to Beth, she looked beautiful. She walked up to the *Tala II* and gave Joshua a hand down.

On the nose, Joshua had already changed their ranks to take into account their meritorious promotions. There was a third kill logo there, too. Capgun had been facetiously pissed, complaining that she'd only gotten the third kill so she could stay on top of the squadron leaderboard.

Five more pilots had gotten two kills in the Battle of Toowoomba, and three of them had been transferred to the new squadrons. It was silly to keep tabs as if it was a competition, but pilots had been doing that since the first ones fired at each other over France with pistols.

"Hey, Ate!"

She turned to see Rocky standing by the rope, a greenshirt holding him back. She walked over and tapped the sailor on the shoulder.

"Hey, he's my brother. Any way you can let him through?"

She looked at Beth's Platinum Star, and recognition broke through.

"We were told to keep all the civilians on that side of the rope, but hell, we enlisted swine got to stick together, right?"

She lifted up the rope, and Rocky passed under it. The *Victory* was a huge ship, and Beth only knew a few of the sailors by sight. She looked at the greenshirt's name tag, cementing it in her memory: Anderson.

"Thanks. I appreciate it.

She led her excited brother up to the *Tala II*. She was glad she'd been able to invite him, all expenses paid by the DSO. She'd hoped her mother would come, but while she'd initially agreed, the thought of leaving the planet's surface to go into space had become too stressful, and she bowed out. Rocky had eagerly taken her place.

"Josh, this is my brother, Rocky," she said, making the introduction.

"Oh, wow. Good to meet you," Josh said. "Hey, you want to sit inside?"

Rocky looked at Beth and asked, "Can I?"

"Knock yourself out," she said with a smile.

One of the greenshirts started to protest when Rocky climbed onto the *Tala II*, but another pulled him back. Not that much taller than Beth, he fit in the cockpit comfortably while Josh leaned in, explaining the layout.

"Satan's balls! These fuckheads can't even handle a Wasp," Mercy said, coming around from behind the _Louhi._ "A big freaking handprint, right on the canopy. I swear—"

She stopped as soon as she saw Rocky in the cockpit.

"Rock!"

Rocky looked up and broke into a beatific smile that set him glowing.

"Excuse me Josh," he said as he scrambled out of the *Tala II*.

He landed with a thump on the deck, then hurried over to them.

"It's so good to finally see you. I know we were supposed to meet at the station, but this is even better."

Mercy reached out to take his hand and gave it a squeeze before dropping it.

"Yes, this is a pleasant surprise. And that," she said, pointing over to her Wasp, "That is the *Louhi*. She's beautiful, isn't she?"

"Not as beautiful as you," "Rock," as Mercy called him, said.

Beth rolled her eyes. Since when was her brother a sweet-talker? She waited for Mercy to spout out some profane rejoinder.

"Oh, you're so sweet, Rock," she said instead.

Beth looked up in shock.

Oh my god, she's blushing!

"All guests not attending the onboard reception, please proceed to the shuttles for transfer back to Charlie Station at this time," a voice filled the hangar.

Seaman Anderson came up and said, "I'm sorry, but you heard the announcement. Your brother's going to have to leave now."

"And we've got to get to the reception here," Beth said. "Go ahead and catch your ride down. We'll meet you at your room in about four hours, OK?"

"Oh, sure. I'll see you both then."

He gave Mercy's hand another squeeze, then gave Beth a hug before he let Seaman Anderson escort him off.

"Who the hell are you, and what did you do with Mercy?" Beth asked.

"What the fuck are you talking about?"

"Oh, you're so sweet, Rock," Beth said dramatically, her voice several octaves higher and mimicking Mercy.

"Well, he is."

"And what happened to your language? You said six sentences, and I didn't hear one f-bomb'"

"Hey, I'm trying to be a little more ladylike, OK?"

"You? Ladylike?"

Mercy laughed, then said, "Yeah, I know. Me, fucking ladylike. I'm giving it a try, though."

They stood together as the greenshirts took the hand mules and started to remove the Wasps.

"It's getting real," Mercy said as they stood side-by-side.

Beth didn't know if she was referring to her and Rocky or the war with the crystals. Probably both.

The task force was commissioned, and it was going to be used. They had a final night of liberty, but at 1200 tomorrow, the task force was departing. They were taking the war to the stars.

Beth put her arm around her friend and said, "Let's go to the reception, then punch out early and get over to Charlie. This might be our last night out for the duration, so make it a good one. For Rocky, too."

Mercy kissed Beth on the forehead, then said, "I intend to. As they say . . ."

In unison, the two wingmates said, "Tonight we party, for tomorrow we may die."

Thank you for reading *Crystals*. I hope you enjoyed the book, and I welcome a review on Amazon, Goodreads, or any other outlet.

If you would like updates on new books releases, news, or special offers, please consider signing up for my mailing list. Your email will not be sold, rented, or in any other way disseminated. If you are interested, please sign up at the link below:

http://eepurl.com/bnFSHH

OTHER BOOKS BY JONATHAN BRAZEE

The Navy of Humankind: Wasp Squadron
Fire Ant
Crystals
Ace

The United Federation Marine Corps
Recruit
Sergeant
Lieutenant
Captain
Major
Lieutenant Colonel
Colonel
Commandant

Rebel
(Set in the UFMC universe.)

Behind Enemy Lines
(A UFMC Prequel)

The Accidental War (A Ryck Lysander Short Story Published in *BOB's Bar: Tales from the Multiverse*)

The United Federation Marine Corps' Lysander Twins
Legacy Marines
Esther's Story: Recon Marine

Noah's Story: Marine Tanker
Esther's Story: Special Duty
Blood United

Coda

<u>Women of the United Federation Marine Corps</u>
Gladiator
Sniper
Corpsman

High Value Target (A Gracie Medicine Crow Short Story)
BOLO Mission (A Gracie Medicine Crow Short Story)
Weaponized Math (A Gracie Medicine Crow Novelette,
Published in *The Expanding Universe 3. Nebula Award Finalist*)

<u>The United Federation Marine Corps' Grub Wars</u>
Alliance
The Price of Honor
Division of Power

<u>Ghost Marines</u>
Integration
Unification
Fusion

<u>The Return of the Marines Trilogy</u>
The Few
The Proud
The Marines

<u>The Al Anbar Chronicles: First Marine Expeditionary Force--Iraq</u>
Prisoner of Fallujah
Combat Corpsman
Sniper

<u>Werewolf of Marines</u>
Werewolf of Marines: Semper Lycanus
Werewolf of Marines: Patria Lycanus
Werewolf of Marines: Pax Lycanus

Soldier

Animal Soldier: Hannibal

To the Shores of Tripoli

Wererat

Darwin's Quest: The Search for the Ultimate Survivor

Venus: A Paleolithic Short Story

Secession

Duty

Semper Fidelis

Checkmate (Published in The Expanding Universe 4)

<u>Non-Fiction</u>

Exercise for a Longer Life

The Effects of Environmental Activism on the Yellowfin Tuna Industry

<u>Author Website</u>

http://www.jonathanbrazee.com

<u>Twitter</u>

https://twitter.com/jonathanbrazee

CPSIA information can be obtained
at www.ICGtesting.com
Printed in the USA
LVHW081007220519
618618LV00033B/905/P